THREE FOR TRINITY

Kevin Major

The author thanks Donna Butt, Artistic Director of Rising Tide Theatre, for her years of friendship and encouragement, and (always the risk-taker!) for agreeing to have a fictional version of herself take centre stage. Well-deserved applause is extended to the dedicated troupe at Breakwater Books, and to editor Marnie Parsons for her unwavering commitment to the script.

BREAKWATER
P.O. Box 2188, St. John's, NL, Canada, A1C 6E6
WWW.BREAKWATERBOOKS.COM

A CIP CATALOGUE RECORD FOR THIS BOOK IS AVAILABLE FROM LIBRARY AND ARCHIVES CANADA

COPYRIGHT ©2021 Kevin Major
ISBN 978-1-55081-914-4

We acknowledge the support of the Canada Council for the Arts. We acknowledge the financial support of the Government of Canada and the Government of Newfoundland and Labrador through the Department of Tourism, Culture, Industry and Innovation for our publishing activities.
PRINTED AND BOUND IN CANADA.

Canada Council   Conseil des Arts   Canadä   Newfoundland
for the Arts   du Canada   Labrador

Breakwater Books is committed to choosing papers and materials for our books that help to protect our environment. To this end, this book is printed on a recycled paper that is certified by the Forest Stewardship Council®.

Bravo, Donna, for your remarkable career in theatre.

She stands before her audience, awkward, serious, her arms failing to find a comfortable position. She's far from her usual effervescent self. Through her clear plastic face shield it is obvious she is distraught. She struggles to show a brave front to this fresh lot of theatregoers who know nothing of what took place a few days before.

An arts icon in Newfoundland, the force behind Rising Tide Theatre for more than thirty years, Donna loves a breezy chat with her audience before a performance. But tonight, while the actors wait to take to the stage, tribute must be paid to the cast member who is no longer part of this summer's troupe.

'Our theatre company each season is family,' Donna tells them. 'That family has lost one of its own, an actor who collapsed on this stage while performing in this very show. Collapsed, and died the following day. We dedicate this performance to the memory of a dear, sweet young man, friend to all who knew him. Lyle, this performance is for you. You'll not be forgotten.'

She exits hurriedly, a hand under the shield, wiping tears as she goes.

A musician strikes up a fiddle, actors make their entrances and Shenanigans *begins. The show must go on.*

What Donna didn't tell the audience is that Lyle was murdered.

His collapse was not the result of drunkenness, as Donna first suspected. Lyle had been dragged away as if his sudden slump over a railing were another comic element in the show. But then, when she rushed backstage to give him a piece of her mind for liquoring up before a performance, she discovered him unconscious and labouring for breath.

'Good God,' she exclaimed. 'Where's his jeesly puffer?' Someone dug it out of Lyle's pants pocket. 'Get him in the back seat of my vehicle, and one of you fellows scravel in there with him.' They headed straight for the hospital in Clarenville. What normally took an hour Donna covered in forty minutes.

Four hours later Lyle was dead. Within twelve hours an autopsy was performed in St. John's. And within two days a toxicology report showed he had inhaled hydrogen cyanide with the marijuana he smoked before he went on stage. Lyle Mercer, with a history of asthma, had suffocated from smoking pot laced with myclobutanil. As Donna said the next time I encountered her, 'In God in heaven's name, how did that get there, however the hell you pronounce it?'

ACT ONE

SCENE 1

WE'LL GET THROUGH IT.

Spring in Newfoundland is never anything but a hopeless wait for warmer weather, but this spring has been a particularly relentless pain in the butt, especially in St. John's, where in January we were buried in a godawful mountain of snow. Eighty centimetres in one day, two and a half feet! What we called Snowmageddon, or effin' Snowmageddon as the state of emergency stretched into eight days.

And then comes COVID, another unrelenting pain in the butt.

"Social distancing" is the rallying cry, but for someone who earns a chunk of his change as a tour guide, it looks like the weeks and weeks of work it took to set the tours in place are about to crash in on themselves. Bookings have come to a screeching halt. And with borders now shut to everything but essential travel, it seems the only scenario possible is a falling-dominoes disaster of cancellations. *On the Rock(s)* looks doomed.

Life has dealt me a dirty hand, and no amount of washing is about to keep disaster at bay.

Isolation has its upside, or so I'm determined to believe.

Somewhere there are fringe benefits to being stuck in the house alone with a mutt. Luckily I have a good stock of Scotch on hand, and a supply of books to keep my whisky blog up and running. *Distill My Reading Heart!* has doubled its daily average of hits. All the way up to ten. Wicked. Way more Scotch lovers inside their respective bubbles keen for recommendations of a good read to go with their dram.

Gaffer loves the home exile. Dog and master all day, every day. No being left alone while the big guy runs off earning a living. Not even any stops during his walks while master chats with neighbours. And, best of all, no strangers showing up in the house kicking dog out of bed so she can have master all to herself.

Son Nick, when he's with me and not my ex, is my break in the routine. As for Nick himself, he's coping as well as can be expected of a fourteen-year-old. At that age existence is all about the social herd, and it takes a while for Group FaceTime to replace banging around with his pals at school. My theory is that his ambivalence was all about the half-dozen full-on headshots staring at each other. Nick spends twenty minutes before every virtual encounter in front of a mirror working his too-long hair so the acne on his forehead is carelessly hidden.

The rule is ninety minutes max of FaceTime, after supper is over and cleanup complete. He gripes and whines of course, though not loud enough to jeopardize his daily overindulgence in texting.

Being an ex-teacher, I know how to crack the whip and keep him focused on the online schoolwork coming his way. Although all schools in the province have shut their doors for the rest of the school year, students are expected to keep up through the glitch-prone power of technology and the prodding of parents. Samantha deals with Language Arts and French, I handle Science, Social Studies, and Health. As for the biggie, Math, the kid is on his own for that one. Math these days is a minefield that neither parent is willing to enter for fear of doing permanent damage.

In recognition of this scholastic state of affairs, Nick makes his way to my place on alternate weekday afternoons for home-schooling sessions. (Plus supper—a concession on the part of my ex, who no doubt relishes the opportunity to have a succession of intimate meals with her live-in.)

A recent focus has been Health, in the broader context. As I knew from ex-colleagues in the teaching profession, the hot topic for Grade Nine Health is "Human Sexuality". I gather from Nick, after considerable prompting, that the teacher was halfway through the unit when the school shut down. Human Sexuality interruptus, so to speak.

I insist I take over the topic, needless to say, against Nick's fervent wishes. 'Dad, man, there's no need. This is ultra-embarrassing. Besides, I know it all.'

'You *know it all*? Enough with the bravado. For what you do know, this will be a refresher.'

I insist, partly because I want to be sure that he knows the basics. I would hate to see his life messed up because there was a gaping hole in his sex ed. And because I figure it has the possibility of adding some much-needed levity to the hours of homeschooling.

'Just fifteen minutes a day, I promise.'

'Oh, God.' A very deep breath.

'Now what was the last topic covered?'

'Sexual orientation,' he says firmly and decisively, hoping to put me off my game.

'Darn, I was counting on that one. I hope the good topics aren't all taken up.'

He doesn't laugh. Not so much as a disgruntled grin.

'Oh well, you got that down pat anyway.'

A bit too offhanded on my part, I decide after the fact. Last year Nick went through a phase when he thought he might be gay. At least that's how we had it figured, that it was a phase.

Nick rolls his eyes before a second, deeper, intake of air.

Hard to read him. Maybe more than a phase? If so, we'll deal with it when he's ready.

Right now I have the Grade Nine Health Curriculum Guide up on my computer screen. 'Ahh, I see next up is *subsection 1.8—methods of preventing pregnancy*. Nice. I think I lucked out after all.'

'Dad, man, this is not going to go well.'

'Let's start with the condom. Should I take it as a given that you know what a condom is?'

'You mean the water balloon thingy?'

'Don't play cute. This is serious business. Now, pay attention. As you might be aware, the condom goes by various names. For example, rubber or French safe.'

'*French* safe? What century was that?'

'Very funny.'

'You're kidding, right? You called it that, back in the day? You mean French, like in the country. Isn't that racist?'

'Okay, wise guy. What name do you dudes have for it?'

'Weanie beanie.'

Scrape me off the floor, why don't you. When I finally stop laughing, he gives me a thumbs-up.

'Got ya. Got ya good.'

From this point on he sits silent and motionless, refusing to show any reaction, except to check the time on his phone every couple of minutes.

A Google search led me to a light-hearted but very informative YouTube animation on how to don a condom. The Sex O'Clock News reporter has an English accent, subtle, but very effective in upping the level of trust.

Discussion remains at a standstill. Fine. 'And now for the IUD.'

'Time's up.'

The fifteen minutes has indeed expired. 'That wasn't so bad.'

Third deep breath.

We work through Human Sexuality over several days. I don't hold back on *subsections 1.9 – 1.11—teen pregnancy*. And as for *subsections 1.12 – 2.2—sexually transmitted infections*, I'll admit I learn a few things myself. Together we conquer both topics, with the added homeschooling advantage that I put the fear of God in him for when his hormones kick in to the max and he starts dating. (If he starts dating. Girls, I mean. Sometimes I'm surprised by my own open-mindedness.)

The completion of the Human Sexuality unit is a good segue into the ritual of making supper.

'Years ago, whenever your mother and I would go to a potluck, someone would invariably show up with a dessert—are you ready for this?—called "sex-in-a-pan".'

'Perverts,' Nick mutters.

Over the last couple of years Nick and I have had some of our best bonding time in the kitchen. I've turned him on to the satisfaction found in cooking a good meal from scratch, not to mention the detour of his palate away from processed food and empty calories.

The odd dessert is the exception. Maybe once a month we'll indulge his (our) craving for something sweet. Today's culinary vice is the aforementioned sex-in-a-pan. An inspired, curriculum-related choice, the ingredients of which I judiciously purchased during my last weekly, face-masked trip to the supermarket.

Butter, cream cheese, vanilla pudding, chocolate pudding, whipped cream, icing sugar, topped with grated chocolate. Okay. There's nutritional salvation—the addition of crushed pecans in the base crust.

When the layered spectacle finally takes its place in the centre of the kitchen table, father and son poised on either side of it, the anticipation is palpable.

Sadly, with the first goopy spoonful its attractiveness begins to waver. By the dishful it has slumped into something neutered and shapeless. Sex-in-a-pan is giving off strange, unbecoming vibes.

'Doesn't look like much but I am sure it will redeem itself.' I recall it had a very solid reputation at church suppers, even though it remained nameless to all but whispering adults. Its reputation may well have been founded on a vague sinfulness.

Sex-in-a-pan has been a bust. One of our very few kitchen losers. There's a life lesson there, somewhere. I'm just not sure how to phrase it.

Yet, good for father-son bonding, if nothing else. When I consider it further, me with my dram, Nick upstairs with his FaceTime show, I take great satisfaction in knowing that the young fellow won't go through life blindly consuming food that's devoid of merit.

Unlike his father. Who up until recently wasn't as cautious as he should have been about what made its way down his gullet. And as a result I bore the burden of a gut. Not a big one, mind you, but sizable enough that I was duly warned by my G.P.—lose twenty pounds or be damned.

Hence, there's twenty pounds less of me and I've slipped seamlessly into a maintenance program. Which means I can occasionally indulge the sweet tooth. (Hence, the dud-in-a-pan.)

A wasted moment of indulgence. The aforementioned dessert (minus six spoonfuls) was promptly dumped in the garbage bin when we cleaned up from supper. I hesitate to endorse food wastage. Then again it didn't really qualify as food.

The dessert debacle is behind us. Case closed.

While I'm checking my email, another reopens. I have girded myself for more news on just how hard the tourism industry has been hit. Instead, what I detect is a flattening of the curve in the cancellations of *On the Rock(s)*. In fact bookings for my new summer tour of the Bonavista Peninsula have suddenly spiked. Like by five people. Mind-boggling.

I look over what's popping up on the screen only to discover they're all names I recognize. All friends of mine. What the hell?

An email from Scotch buddy Jeremy clears the fog.

Looks like Newfoundland and Labrador might move to Alert Level 2 in a few weeks. Yeah! But, even with the promise of an Atlantic Bubble, we're playing it safe and all vacationing at home this year. What better way to do it than together with you! The only qualification for signing up is that we all be champions of the mighty dram! We're looking forward to what you'll have on offer, and of course we'll all be bringing our own. Cheers!

I'm stunned. These guys, who likely know the Bonavista Peninsula better than I do, are putting cash on the table to help a friend through this rough patch in the road. As if they haven't got better uses for their money. I'm touched to the core.

That accounts for four of the recognizable names. There's another on the newly invigorated list. Not sure I could call her a friend. Rather, an acquaintance whom I came to know briefly last fall in my other role in life. That of private investigator. We did come to the point of sharing drams of the Macallan. That spoke volumes.

Ailsa Bowmore. Inspector Ailsa Bowmore of the Royal Canadian Mounted Police. We got along rather well at the time. I like to imagine there's another reason she would sign up for the tour, other than having a taste for Scotch.

Together with the late entry from Nova Scotia, the only original participant who didn't get caught up in the stampede to cancellation. And who will now be part of said Atlantic Bubble, allowing unrestricted travel from the other three Atlantic provinces.

A full roster of six eager participants.

Let the COVID Level 2 expanded, maskless bubble take shape. Let *On the Rock(s)* unfold. There's an intrepid, tireless leader who in mid-August will make it happen.

SCENE 2

THERE ARE DAYS when Newfoundland astounds me. Its sheer natural beauty quickened by the unrelenting thrust of the North Atlantic.

Take Cape Bonavista. Day one, first stop of the tour, a stunner of an opening act. No wonder explorer Giovanni Caboto seized on it as his landing site in 1497. Bloody well blown away by the landscape, he knew it was futile to go further. He knew tourist industry planners would forever curse him if he did.

Take Champney's West. Take the hiking trail and be struck speechless when you come upon the slice of rock that shapes Fox Island. Cross the isthmus to it, ascend its grassy fields and the view from the summit will leave you weak in the knees. It's too late in the year for icebergs, but just imagine, I tell them, an immense slice of glacial ice vying for your attention. 'You wouldn't get your breath back long enough to depress the shutter.'

Take Elliston, at the edge of its puffin colony. Enough said. Here I just stand back and let the topography do the talking.

They seem happy enough without the chatter. I find a

rock to sit on, and wait to see who's the first to be slowly but surely overwhelmed. Adam it is, even if it takes place through the lens of his Nikon.

Adam has been Jeremy's partner for two months now. That works for me. Jeremy needed someone in his life, and except for his unrelenting thirst for the exceptional photograph, Adam seems the perfect match. They share a love of travel, Japanese food, jazz, and Scotch, to name only the basic requirements if they are to get along. Jeremy can be funny as hell sometimes. Adam less so, but he's working on it.

As for the other couple, Todd and Jillian, I've known the male half since university residence days. Todd and I shared a room for two years, during the second of which I started dating Samantha. Todd, the indispensable sounding board.

He and I have stayed friends, off and on, ever since. Through a lot. His split with his first wife. My split with Sam, which proved a hard go, pretty tension-driven. He and Jillian have been able to do what I would have thought impossible—remain friends with both of us. Todd and I maybe more so, but they keep contact with Sam, and as far as I can tell at least, it's working. They've set limits. I don't discuss my ex-wife in front of them, and she doesn't discuss me.

I look at them sitting together on a rock (with binoculars, not cameras) and I have to admire the relationship they've settled into. What is it, other than luck and a willingness to compromise? Patience? I thought about it a lot during the months of lockdown. Alone and verging on feeling sorry for myself.

Quick to nip that mind warp in the bud. Though not before a period of fixation on the fact that Sam had found a zealous replacement for me, in record time. One Frederick Olsen. *Inspector* Frederick Olsen of the Royal Newfoundland Constabulary.

Which leads me to Inspector Ailsa Bowmore. First introduced to me by Frederick. (Or Fred, as son Nick is wont to call
him, given they inhabit the same house when Nick is not with
me.) Last year the pair of inspectors shared a case in which I
played, shall we say, a pivotal role. With broken ribs (now firmly
healed) to prove it.

The "inspector" title is, of course, dropped during the tour.
In fact, I make no mention of her being in the RCMP. It does
come out in the course of casual conversation that she works in
law enforcement, but she adeptly sidesteps her exact position.
She's on holiday and wants to leave her work life behind.
Which suits me just fine. I'm interested in coming to know this
woman without the image of her in a scarlet tunic, packing a
Smith & Wesson.

As for the final shareholder in the *On the Rock(s)* "More
than Justa Vista" tour of the Bonavista Peninsula, there's not a
great deal to be said about Alistair McDuff. To be kind, he has
a little trouble focusing for extended periods on the landscape.
It would seem whisky, far more than the vistas, is what drew
him to the tour. No surprise, given the Scottish bent of his
name, and the fact that he showed up well-stocked, shall we
say. He's eager to share, which allows us to overlook the fact
that by the end of each day of the tour he's quietly pickled. The
fellow has a tendency to nod off about ten each evening.

Alistair has proven to be the icebreaker. The other six of us
have all had our "Alistair moments", as we have come to call
them. His impromptu rendition of "Comin' thro' the Rye", after
a sustained encounter with a whisky by the name of Ghleann
Dubh, being the most memorable. Alistair has a fondness for
"Rabbie" Burns, his ancestors (as he proudly revealed) having
come from Scotland and all.

It should be noted that the Dark Glen (translated on the
bottle for those of us not versed in the Gaelic tongue) was an

unqualified success all around. It's a Canadian peated whisky (in itself, an oxymoron). The other lads and I were a bit skeptical, adoring smoky Scotch as we do.

The first whisky offering being a sizable hit is a relief, given it was my idea (in keeping with the vacation-at-home vibe of the tour) that we limit our consumption to whiskies distilled in our home and native land. A little resistance at first from the two Scotch fanatics, but finally they took up the challenge, with an eagerness to do their part to help reboot the Canadian economy in these COVID times.

Pike Creek 21-year-old Oloroso Sherry Cask Finish (a mouthful in more ways than one) is Ailsa's offering. Very good choice, Ailsa.

Surnames are quickly dispensed with on tour, and it's amazing how easily conversation flows when she's in a sweatshirt and jeans, sitting around a firepit. I've come to see a whole different side of the woman.

'More than ample on the front end,' says Jeremy. 'Lovely balance.' The richness of his initial taste of the whisky comes as something of a surprise.

'Indeed,' adds Todd. 'Terrific mouth feel. You can really lose yourself in this one.'

'I'm getting orange zest,' I inject.

'Peppery caramel.'

'Oaky hit of figs.'

'Crème brûlée.'

'Of course, crème brûlée. How could I have missed friggin' crème brûlée?' Alistair mutters dryly. He's not big on specifics. Either he likes it or he doesn't. A thumbs-up in this case.

Ailsa is pleased. 'I grew up in Windsor. Had to make my choice homegrown.'

Despite her Ontario city background, it would seem Ailsa has a deep-seated attraction to nature. She thrives in the

outdoors, as I witnessed this morning when we hiked the coastline loop of the Skerwink Trail. There are a few stiffly uphill
sections, but no sweat for Ailsa, who would have gladly hiked
it a second time had that been an option.

The Skerwink makes for an extraordinarily scenic five
kilometres. Swooping eagles and sea stacks set against azure
blue water are alone worth the price of admission. By the end,
however, Alistair was out of gas and thirsting for the promised
stop at the local craft brewery. Tour guiding is nothing if not
a balancing act. Fit versus unfit. Scenic stop versus beverage
stop. Five of them versus Alistair. This time around I'm blessed
with a flexible group, which has not always been the case. The
others are willing to accommodate the Alistair moments. At this
point at least, with eye-rolling as warranted.

Port Rexton Brewing is another of Newfoundland's outport
breweries that has been a resounding success. In a regular
summer they can hardly keep up with the traffic, but this
summer being notably irregular we're cheered to find outdoor
seating for all seven of us together, adjacent to the brewery's
permanent food truck, Oh My Cheeses. I take it they don't
cater to church suppers.

Offbeat gourmet grilled cheese sandwiches, together with a
round of IPA from the brewery, and we're set for a lip-smacker
of a lunch.

'Right up there with haggis, neeps, and tatties,' says Alistair
later, when we're sitting outside at the tour's home base, the
upscale saltbox I've rented in Bonavista.

Jeremy stares at him from across the firepit. A mere eye-
roll won't do. 'You're fakin' it, Alistair, ol' man. When is the
last time you had jeesly haggis?' Jeremy is on his third dram of
Crown Royal Northern Harvest.

'I was reared on haggis.'

Everyone chuckles, Jeremy the loudest of all. 'And neeps

and tatties,' he says. 'By God, don't be forgetting the neeps and tatties.'

Alistair is not the least offended. He laughs wildly. 'That, too.'

All part of his persona. I've concluded that Alistair has forged a character for himself and uses it to make his way through life, a life which, by the look of him, has handed out more than a few smacks in the gut. As far as he's concerned, the rest of the world can take him or leave him. Or go to blue blazes, as my father used to say.

Alistair says nothing more, just smiles broadly and pours himself another dram.

Jeremy shakes his head, hands Alistair a crooked smile, and does the same.

'Grassy earthiness.'

'Sun-dried linen with a tempting whiff of smoke.'

'Charismatic, but charismatic without being cliché.'

'It's no Bruichladdich, but then again, what is?'

Alistair is first off to bed. But not far behind are the two couples, leaving Ailsa and myself to shoot what breeze remains. I'll admit to being slightly off my game. As much as I would prefer it otherwise, when I look across to the Adirondack chair that holds this woman, I find it impossible to separate the person from the cop.

She senses it. Before she says anything, I get up and move to the empty chair next to her. The fire has died down, perhaps past the time to add another log. I lean back, looking up at the sky.

'*It's a braw bricht moonlicht nicht the nicht,*' she says.

I glance at her. Haven't got a sweet clue.

'It's a bright moon out tonight.'

'Aye.'

She chuckles. 'The distillery pronunciation was quite good

overall. I was impressed.'

'I take it there's room for improvement.'

'Bruichladdich. Your "Brook-laddie" is close, but the "Bruich" needs a little tweaking.'

So. We've loosened up a bit. Or I've loosened up and she was already there.

I toss another log on the fire.

And several more over the course of the next couple of hours. I learn she has also divorced in the recent past. A shorter marriage than my own, and no kids. She's a runner, loves canoeing, and brews her own beer. She's a lapsed Catholic and a lapsed yogi. She's bilingual and has been known to read crime novels in the original French.

Having lapsed on several fronts myself, I note we do have some important things in common. Including a love of Scotch and a fondness for new food adventures.

'Actually I'm a better baker than I am a cook.'

'And you make your own bread, right?'

'On occasion.'

'You remember Nick. We spend a lot of time in the kitchen, experimenting with ingredients.'

'Good for you. I'm envious.'

'We'll invite you over for a meal sometime.'

'I'd love that. I'll bring dessert.'

There it is. Awkward next step reached. I'm tempted to tell her to bring dessert but leave her Smith & Wesson behind. Just for a joke. I think better of it.

Prime tour day tomorrow. Focus on Trinity. Sea kayaking. Jaunt around town in the afternoon, theatre in the evening.

We both need our sleep. I pour water on the embers, literally not figuratively.

No, it's been good. I'm cool. We'll see each other in the morning.

SCENE 3

THE TOWN OF Trinity and the places surrounding it are some of the most lens-worthy in all of Newfoundland. Adam has a field day.

Settler history here goes back to the 1500s. Site of the first court of justice in the New World. Site of the first smallpox vaccination in that same new world, the local doctor being a pal of Edward Jenner. Not only that, in Trinity you can get a good cup of coffee, which is not always the case in rural Newfoundland.

In plenty of ways Trinity is far from your typical outport. In summer the homes are filled with transient townies and mainlanders; in winter the population dwindles to a resolute handful of permanent residents.

It's a tourist town, a bit too picture perfect, no longer so authentically rural. But hey, don't knock it for thriving when the weather and ingenuity of the people are in tandem. Rising Tide Theatre alone normally employs some forty people over the course of its summer season. Trinity helps drive the economy of the whole Bonavista Peninsula and for that alone it's got to be admired.

I've been here several times over the years. Have not gone sea kayaking before, however. Never been much interested in sea kayaking, or kayaking in general for that matter. But in this business you cater to other people's interests, even though they might not always align with your own. When a tour has been filled, I assess the potential passions and physical limitations of the group and insert an optional extra something into the program.

In this case, instead of a morning admiring the views of the saltwater from the beach at Trinity, we're off in a Zodiac, four tandem kayaks in tow, to a more rugged section of the coastline and the chance of getting up close and comfortable with . . . yes . . . whales.

The party of six are all keen. Alistair a bit less so, but one thing Alistair doesn't want is to be left behind when the rest of us are in on the action. He's paid his money, he wants the full meal deal.

Owner and operator Jack beaches the Zodiac and we take to the kayaks. Two of the pairings are obvious. I suggest novice Alistair is safer with expert Jack, which leaves me in the middle of the fourth boat with the kayak-savvy Ailsa in the stern. Nicely executed on my part.

We've lucked into a calm, clear morning, the sun glinting on a scattering of sea stacks and small, craggy islands. There's a striking stone arch leading into a shallow cave. Ailsa manoeuvres about with ease. She obviously downplayed her kayak experience, and I am game to be outclassed, so we're getting along rather well. It takes a while to get my stroke down pat, but once I have it, it's all a matter of practice.

In any case, focus on my paddle rhythm is suddenly overshadowed by the sighting, by sharp-eyed Jack, of the dorsal fin of a humpback whale. I know the feeling, embedded in every tour group leader—the relief, the rush from knowing that what your participants are all hoping for is suddenly about to unfold. Jack takes dead aim with his kayak and is off in the direction of one of the mammoths of the animal kingdom.

Fortunately, expert that he is, Jack is very good at compensating for Alistair's hopeless paddle rhythm. On the bright side, Alistair's steep learning curve allows the remaining three pairs of paddlers to catch up. We all arrive at roughly the same time, thrillingly close to the whale. The view is from a safe distance, but stunning nonetheless.

There are levels of humpback experience. There's the basic skim just above the surface of the water, the dorsal fin show. There's the more full-bodied skim, an awesome view of the whale's overall size. There's the dive and brilliant show of tail, revealing a splendid pair of v-notched flukes. Then there's every whale watcher's dream—the breach! In which the whale thrusts itself up and out of the water, towering to an unbelievable 80-90% of crustacean-encrusted mass before landing with a humungous splash. And finally, the mother of all shows— the double breach!! In which two magnificent mammoths lunge from the water in unison and land with a thunderous, gob-smacking, almighty wallop of water!

Needless to say, the last such occurrence is hopelessly rare. The chances of seeing it close to zilch. Still, it happens. And in Newfoundland waters. I've seen the video.

We have our moment. First a decent tail. Then, several minutes later, a breach of roughly 60%.

Wow! I find the word is very much overused these days. But this definitely fits the experience. Wow!

I've whale-watched from a boat with fifty other people, but at sea level in a kayak it is definitely a more intimate freaking experience. Man might think of himself as king of the universe, but when a 15-metre / 30,000-kilogram cetacean breaks the same surface as his ultra-lightweight kayak, even at the regulation distance of 100 metres, it takes him down a decisive notch or two.

Alistair, in the kayak closest to us, is looking like the staff of God has poked him in the chest. Adam snaps a portrait for posterity, before pivoting back to the expanse of water where the whale last made an appearance.

It would seem the humpback is moving off, having fulfilled its contract with the provincial department of tourism. Only Alistair is showing signs of relief. For any of the group who might have the proverbial bucket list, the check mark has pierced the paper on which it's written.

The whole gang has been released from its collective trance and gives way once again to conversation. This is where a tour leader would like to have the audacity to videotape the comments, store them for later retrieval and insertion in his online tour description. They are promotional gold.

I should not be so crass. Instead I should be revelling in how the experience has solidified our little troupe, set us up for the rest of the day, knowing that whatever happens from here on in, I have an awesome breach of cetacean to fall back on.

Ashore in Trinity, sitting around the restaurant table, we're having trouble focusing on the menu of the Dock Marina. It's all whale talk until the waitress returns for a second time to take our order. Quick decision—fish and chips all around. Menu closed, and back to the whale.

Adam nailed some definitive moments, and, though it takes flicking through dozens of images to get to it, he did hit the motherlode—the hefty beast at its peak out of the water, arched, at the pivotal point before the freefall. (Continuous shooting mode is a godsend, of course, but let's not quibble.) Within a few minutes the image is in all our inboxes. A chain of contentment circles the table. It does a tour guide's heart good. Adam wins again.

The afternoon brings us back into the thick of "More than Justa Vista". No rest for the eager half-dozen. Since 1993 Rising Tide's anchor event has been an outdoor performance piece, a theatrical walk about Trinity that interprets the history of the town, what it calls the *New Founde Lande Pageant*. I've seen it before, yet it never fails to entertain and at times brings a few of the audience to tears. Humour and tragedy is always a tough duo, more so in an outdoor setting, but these actors are a well-seasoned lot. They have come together to form their own bubble, unmasked when in performance.

The *Pageant* finishes up with the singing of the "Ode to Newfoundland", our anthem when this fair isle was its own country, and still sung long after we threw in the towel and cast our lot with Canada in 1949. Talk about stirring love for this place.

It has started to rain on the actors on the hillside and the audience below, but no one is going anywhere, mainlanders included, until the final verse is sung, the *Pageant* reaching its emotional apex. Well done, you crowd. It eases into a sustained round of applause.

'What say we head to Rocky's?'

Leave it to Alistair to break the mood. Alistair is not feeling anything except thinly disguised relief that it's finally over. The priorities of his central nervous system are not easily altered.

I saw him talking to a couple of the actors between scenes, no doubt sniffing out the beverage possibilities in town. Rocky's is Trinity's lone bar, and the reality is we could do with a little downtime before the start of the theatre performance. Alistair gladly leads the way.

Rocky's has seen better days. There have been Saturday nights when it was packed to the rafters, live music clogging the dance floor until two in the morning, the ex-Synard couple among the sweaty lot. A past life better set aside.

At the moment there's us, a pair of young fellows playing pool, and a senior citizen feeding quarters into a VLT. Plus the young woman behind the bar. We're the only non-locals she's seen all afternoon. A bit of a flourish for her.

I scan the limited selection of what my father's generation called hard liquor. My guess is a single malt has never landed anywhere near the shelf. Whisky is out of the picture.

Unless, that is . . . 'Who's game to revisit the whisky virgin years of their youth?'

It cracks them up. 'You're kidding?'

'Rye and ginger, or, better yet, rye and seven.'

'Only if it comes with ketchup chips,' says Todd, hitting the sweet spot in our collective memories of cabin parties.

'And pickled eggs,' says Alistair, whose youth was obviously more adventuresome than our own.

We're around a table then (wobbly until someone sticks a wad of cardboard under one leg), drinks in hand. That would be Canadian Club and Canada Dry, or Royal Reserve and 7UP, over glassfuls of ice cubes. The ketchup chips have sold out, but there are plenty of bags of that other perennial Newfoundland chip-flavour of choice—roast chicken. No pickled eggs, but a plate of pickled wieners, yes indeed. Something to tide us over until later tonight. Rather than supper before the show, we've opted for a barbecue when we get back to Bonavista.

'Where's Jon Bon Jovi when we need him,' declares Jillian.

'You, too?' says Ailsa, and the two of them spontaneously break into the wailing chorus of *Livin' On A Prayer*.

'Killer!' shouts Todd, as we all might have shouted at the time, longer ago than any of us care to remember.

'The glory days,' I put out there, evoking Springsteen, main man of my angst-prone youth.

'All days are glory days,' says Alistair.

The man has a story to tell.

'*We're Here For A Good Time (Not A Long Time)*.'

Right on, Alistair. And right on cue the other six of us hit the Trooper biggie dead on.

Deeply embedded in the soundtrack of every Canadian kid who lost his virginity in the 1980s. That wouldn't have been Alistair, unless he was a late bloomer. In any case it's a slick lead-in to something from his storied past.

'Not a long time, remember that. As it is, I figure I'm on borrowed time.'

I ask for date of birth when people sign up for a tour, in case there's a medical emergency. Alistair might look like he's been around the block a few times too many, but he's only 61, as of last May. Hardly borrowed time for the average Joe.

'Cancer,' he says. 'Smoked since I was fifteen. Gave it up, but a bit too late. In remission, though, for the past year. That's the good news.'

All news to me, which it shouldn't be. As I recall, the medical history section on the sign-up form was blank, except for three words. "Good to go."

He didn't specify how far. Alistair looks over at me. 'Couldn't take a chance on being turned down.'

In my head is a scene where he's collapsed on the Skerwink Trail, struggling for breath, another two kilometres to get back to the vehicle. Could have been an ugly episode.

The reality is he's here now, and by the way he ambles off to the washroom, no worse for wear. A well-practised round of eye-rolling in his absence. In reference no doubt to the fact he's given up cigarettes, but is still game for a joint, as we've all witnessed over the past few evenings.

It's his life, as they say. Fortunately, the walk/hike components of the tour are behind us. By this time tomorrow he'll be on his way back home to Nova Scotia, in no worse shape than when he arrived. Hopefully.

We still have an hour to kill before the start of the show. Adam and Jeremy are off for a walk to parts of Trinity that might have escaped Adam's lens. There are some craft stores that we passed earlier in the afternoon that Jillian and Ailsa decide to check out. Which leaves Todd and me to figure what we'll do to escape an hour alone with Alistair.

As it turns out, no such dilemma. As Alistair exits the washroom, he stops momentarily, glances over at the table, and checks his watch. 'See you at the theatre, gentlemen. I'm off to commune with nature.' He stiffly shifts direction and is out the door.

No need to debate the turn of phrase. Alistair, we both conclude, is in need of weed to invigorate his evening and up his remission risk factor.

For us it's time to ourselves. Todd and I go back further than any of the others. We started university the same year, naïve 18-year-olds, me from Gander, Todd from Twillingate. Ended up in res, as we called it, roommates in Bowater House. A hundred males in the place, long before it turned co-ed. Looking back on it, two of the best years of our lives. Nothing like being crammed together in an eight-by-twelve-foot room to test a friendship. We survived, thrived in fact. Smoked up, learned to drink and puke with the best of them, had more than our share of laughs, managed to get laid, and passed all our courses at the same time.

'Remember the time . . .' We go to half a dozen places firmly ingrained in our collective memories, filling up the better part of the hour until the women return and wonder why we're laughing so hard.

Not for sharing. It's time to move off. The theatre calls.

SCENE 4

IT'S BEEN A tough few months for Rising Tide. With tourists from outside Atlantic Canada shut out of the province, there was no choice but cut back the season—stage fewer shows with smaller casts, and rework the audience size and seating to adhere to government COVID guidelines for performance spaces. Which means, instead of a hundred or more patrons on a good night, any show is down to half that number. At best. Pockets of stay-at-home vacationers mostly, masked groupings scattered through the tiered seating, what you might call "audience bubbles".

In seasons past Donna Butt, the woman behind Rising Tide's success story, would be there to greet folks as they arrived for the show. Old friends or people she'd never laid eyes on before, she would have time for them all. That's out of the question this season. She's off to one side, her ample arms folded, a plastic shield curved around her face, trying not to look like the world has fallen down around her.

A few years back, in the months after I quit teaching, I landed a short-term job at the Arts and Culture Centre in St. John's. Donna came through for a four-night run of *Revue*, a show she tours annually in the off-season. We got to know each other. Let's just say she's not someone you soon forget.

I stride to within two metres of her. It's a hell of a struggle not to wrap our arms around each other.

'Look what the cat dragged in! Sebastian, my love, whataya at?'

You have to know Donna to appreciate her humour. Nobody is above a good-natured jibe. She thrives on spirited banter, all the more so with someone she hasn't seen in a while.

'Shag all. Figured I'd come out, take in a couple of shows, unload some hard-earned cash.'

'Cough once and you're out the friggin' door! No refund.' She bellows with laughter, which doesn't have quite the usual impact from behind a shield. 'Don't be talkin', Sebastian. What a racket. If I had my time back I would have shut 'er down before we started, barred the door, and gone home out of it.'

Not likely. Donna is an arts warrior if there ever was one. She's fought through countless crises over the years. Some would say she thrives on them. Though, granted, this one is tougher than most.

Don't stay calm, but carry on. It could be her motto.

'I got a tour business on the go,' I tell her. 'Got a gang of six taking in your show tonight.'

'Now you're talkin'!'

'*On the Rock(s)* I call it. "The Rock", like in Newfoundland; "Rocks", like in whisky.'

'On the rocks is right. We're all on the friggin' rocks!'

Before she has the chance to enliven our banter even more, Donna is called away to handle some dispute about a couple from Witless Bay wanting to join up with a couple from Come By Chance, apparently old friends who haven't seen each other in years. 'Not allowed.' Her voice trails away from us as she heads into the fray. 'Stay within the bubble you booked. That's the rule. I'm sorry, folks, no spontaneous double-bubbling.'

She does her level best to stay civil and disarm the situation, though her face shield is likely steaming up with frustration at an attempted circumventing of the regulations. The last thing she can chance is a government shutdown of the theatre and a cut to her arts grant. She's barely surviving as it is.

As our group assembles and dutifully heads to our assigned seating, we can see a truce has been reached. Donna has the final word. 'Burst whatever bubble you want after the show. Once you're off the property I'm no longer responsible. Enjoy yourselves, folks.' When she turns away her smile hardens, and no doubt vanishes once she's out of range of the audience.

All of whom are now seated and ready for the show to begin.

A prerequisite for being hired by Rising Tide is that you be multi-talented. If you can't sing or play an instrument you'd better darn well have something else besides acting up your sleeve. Donna has a part for you in *Shenanigans*, the evening variety show, regardless of the fact you're beat out after just spending two hours parading around Trinity in the sun and wind as part of the *Pageant*.

With the season's company reduced, it seems only the cream of the crop has been hired. They are an amazingly talented lot, merging seamlessly between the roaring opening musical number—fiddle, accordion, and voices in high gear— to a recitation called "Gutted by COVID", composed just for the show, to a skit, based on a Ted Russell yarn from the years before Confederation, called "The Hangashore".

The Newfoundland word "hangashore" needs an explanation, which is forthcoming from one of the characters before they're long into the skit. A good-for-nothing, a slacker, someone too lazy to fish, who'd rather stay ashore and cause trouble. I couldn't rightly call Alistair a hangashore, but he does have some of the traits.

In this case the hangashore is Solomon Noddy. In he comes from stage left, looking every bit the part in a check shirt and overly wide tie, a mismatch for the plaid jacket and baggy pants. He's unsteady on his feet, looking like he hit the bottle one too many times, very definitely gone to seed. Edging toward the farcical. His dialect is slurred and not decipherable by the audience, even though we're mostly Newfoundlanders.

He's taken a seat in a courtroom, behind a railing, and is just about to hear the charge of theft. He squares himself up, prepared to lay out a defence. Suddenly, without warning, Solomon Noddy collapses. He hangs illogically over the railing.

The audience roars.

His only movement is the heave of his chest generated by a prolonged round of coughing. The audience laughter comes to an abrupt end. The infectious perils of open coughing have been so ingrained in us over the past several months that everyone instantly checks that their face masks are secure. The audience bubbles seated closest to the stage stiffen, prepared to retreat.

The most theatre-savvy among us are wondering if what happened is not all part of the skit. Solomon Noddy is unceremoniously dragged offstage, causing a few people to chuckle tentatively. But then the storyline falls apart. The remainder of the cast stands mute and miserable, clueless about what to do next.

And tearing her way from the back of the theatre where she's been watching the performance is Donna, hair flying, sputtering behind her face shield so intensely that it fogs her view of the audience. She abruptly snatches it away.

'Sorry about that folks. No need to worry. He's been tested. They've all been tested. It's his asthma. Probably mislaid his puffer. You know what the young crowd is like. Sit back, folks, enjoy the rest of the show. Meanwhile I'll make sure he's okay.'

Which is meant as much for the cast left onstage as it is for the audience. The space is cleared of the skit's props in record time. Donna is hardly out of sight before the fiddle is back in action, displacing the pall that had pervaded the theatre. The show goes on. These things happen.

I glance at Ailsa. She's also not so sure. She leans close to my ear. 'I think I better check this out.'

She abandons her seat, the tour guide behind her, both of us trying to look inconspicuous as we take the same side entrance to backstage that Donna had taken.

We hear her before we reach the cluster of people around Solomon Noddy, who by this time has finally stopped coughing. 'Good God. Where's his jeesly puffer? Lyle, if you're drunk I'll have your friggin' head.' We watch as one of the stagehands digs the inhaler out of Lyle's pants pocket.

Ailsa steps forward. 'I'm trained as a first responder.' Donna snaps a look at her, but before there's time to ask the question, Ailsa flashes her identification card. 'Inspector Bowmore. RCMP.'

'She's part of my tour group,' I add quickly.

'Move back, boys. Give her room.' An RCMP officer can have that effect.

Ailsa kneels on the floor next to Lyle. Makes a quick check of his pulse. Forces open each eyelid. Rests a hand on his chest. Puts her own face closer to his. She glances up at Donna. 'Heart rate is good, but his pupils are constricted and his breathing is abnormal. You should get him to a hospital right away.' Adding as an afterthought, 'No smell of alcohol on his breath.'

It sets Donna in high gear. 'Get him in the back seat of my vehicle,' she barks, tossing a ring of keys in the direction of a stagehand. 'And one of you fellows scravel in with him.'

Soon they're gone, out a back door and around the side of

the theatre to her 4Runner, now spitting gravel as it backs up the access road and tears off in the direction of the Clarenville hospital, seventy kilometres away, no mind to the fact that an RCMP officer is staring into the trail of dust.

For Ailsa and me there's nothing to do but make our way through the main entrance and back into the theatre. We wait there until, during a round of applause between items on the program, we return to our seats.

The applause is not what it had been. There is uncertainty in the air, and try as they might to conceal it, the performers look just as relieved as the audience when the bows are over and *Shenanigans* ends.

"More than Justa Vista" takes to the van and heads back to its accommodation. 'That was a bit of excitement,' says Jeremy, digging for more of what went on backstage. 'Donna must have been freaking.'

Better not to go there. 'Fortunately Ailsa qualifies as a first responder,' I tell them.

They might be impressed, but what they're really after is the inside scoop. 'The fellow looked drunk to me,' says Adam. 'As soon as he came on stage, I figured he had one too many.'

'Not necessarily,' offers Ailsa. She adds nothing beyond that, her police instincts having kicked in.

'High,' says Jeremy. 'Then he was definitely high.'

They need something to relieve their thirst. 'His asthma didn't help,' I put out there. 'He possibly had an allergic reaction.'

Now they're all in on it, given that Jillian is an RN. 'I'd rule out anaphylactic shock,' she says decisively.

'At least he didn't vomit,' inserts Todd, not wanting to be left out of the speculation. 'We can take that as a positive.'

The only one silent is Alistair. His dearth of medical knowledge is a plus. I'm more than happy not having to deal with

Alistair's arbitrary hunches. Small mercies.

By the time we reach Bonavista, Lyle Mercer has been diagnosed with any number of conditions, up to and including mental breakdown due to the stress of a love affair gone bad. Jeremy has what I hope is the final word as I park the van. 'You know actors. They're a volatile lot.'

Let's just leave it at that, shall we. The tour is wrapping up tomorrow and I'm determined to go out on a bright and eager note.

The seven of us are gathered around the firepit, having tucked contentedly into charred ribs and veggies. Dram of Caldera Champlain in one hand and dark, succulent chocolate in the other.

'I'm thinking drug overdose.'

Good God. Go back to taking pictures, Adam. Do the world a favour.

'I wouldn't count it out,' inserts Jeremy. 'You know actors.'

Actors and their medical histories. Their knowledge base is extraordinary. 'Back to the matter at hand, folks.' I try not to sound like I'm cutting them off at the pass, but that's exactly my objective.

'Very smooth.' It's Ailsa to the rescue. 'Goes wonderfully well with the chocolate.'

'You know what I think.' I take my time, drawing it out, more determined than ever to reposition the focal point. 'Time measured in refined moments, a sublime touch of whisky bringing your day to an unimaginable close. Your world suddenly centred on the essence of fermentation you hold in your hand, the discord of the cosmos drifting into firelight.'

'Jesus,' murmurs Alistair.

'That's quite the tasting note,' says Adam.

'Are you sure it's not just whisky?' chuckles Todd. 'Did you see God in the process?'

They all have their laugh, but that's okay. Mission accomplished.

'Who's for a refill? Don't hold back. Last night together, make it memorable.'

Alistair stands up and hands me his empty glass. 'That's it for me, folks.' It's the most he's said since we sat around the fire.

'Alistair, man, it's the last night. You can't be crashing yet,' says Jeremy.

Alistair stands his ground. He says nothing more, raising his hand in a departing gesture, then disappears inside.

'An odd duck,' notes Adam.

But harmless, which is more than I can say of some who've signed up for *On the Rock(s)* in the past. Everyone has their idiosyncrasies, maybe whisky fiends more than most.

The lads are looking like they need their peat.

They have stayed patriotic Canadians almost to the end, but there's no denying their inclinations any longer. Jeremy pulls from a knapsack something unmistakably whisky-box sized, wrapped in brown paper, "in case of emergency" scrawled across it in black marker.

He hands it to Todd, who hands it to me. 'To celebrate a killer tour, Sebastian. You do the honours. From your tour group. To you.' Pause. 'To share.'

Broad smiles. There is no wondering what it could be, only what label it bears. The six of them might have thrown in the bucks, but there's no doubt these two guys were the ones to track down the whisky.

I tear away the brown paper, to reveal a box, dark and lurid. 'Good God. Compass Box blend. This has been on my wish list forever. You're kidding me.'

The Peat Monster. The fucking Peat Monster. As I would have said if it were just the three of us.

I'm touched. I've never been anywhere that I could put my

hands on a bottle. I look over at the pair of them, my drinking buddies for years. 'You guys, you're too much. Where did you get it?'

'We have our ways.'

Jillian is not into smoke. Ailsa is all for giving it a go. Adam plays along. But for the whisky trio this blend of Laphroaig and Caol Ila is heaven. We suck into it like demons.

Ailsa sips and smiles through it, but is likely thinking it's overkill. She's probably right. But the dram is all in the anticipation, three fellows who've been through a lot together and managed to stay friends all these years. Whisky our common denominator.

Glasses raised high. 'Cheers, everyone.'

Ailsa takes it up a notch. '*Here's tae us. Wha's like us? Damn few, and they're a' deid!*'

Not a clue.

'Here's to us. Who's as good as us? Damn few, and they're all dead.'

I like this woman.

A lot. As evidenced by the extra hour, with just the two of us, the fire fading to embers.

And when it's time to say good night, as much as I'm wondering if it could be more, there is an embrace, a well-mannered kiss on the lips.

Yes, I can be a gentleman and feel good about myself. I can put my weeks and weeks of COVID-drought aside, and extend the wish that she sleep well as we start toward our bedrooms for the remainder of the night.

Okay.

Slow the pace of deceit. How about I take a breath and face it. As noble as it might sound, I'm a fraud. This man has but one thing on his mind.

Likewise, the woman who is still only a few metres away. To

judge by the fact that I do not hear the turn of a doorknob.

I glance back and meet her looking at me. Slow, mutual admission. Not particularly embarrassing.

I follow her into the room and close the door behind me. There is barely enough light coming through the window to discern the bed.

It is all the light we need.

By morning, in the shower, I make a point of having other things on my mind. Such as what's ahead in order to get the van packed and everyone on the road at a decent hour.

Only over a cup of uninspiring coffee do I succumb. Might it not be a good thing to become romantically involved with an officer of the RCMP? Considering my other mode of employment. Can falling in love amount to a conflict of interest?

Fortunately, the others begin to emerge from their respective bedrooms, joining me at the table. Indeed, the questionable coffee becomes a very good reason to be packing up and moving on.

We're off, backtracking to our former lives. Often at this stage of a tour, conversation lags and the partygoers show signs of what I call "the tour hangover" as they settle into thinking what faces them on the return to home base. I glance in the rearview mirror and see that Alistair has claimed a section of the rear seat and fallen back to sleep, his hangover especially potent.

We're nearing Clarenville, heading to the Trans-Canada. Ailsa, who, at the insistence of the others (wink, wink; nudge, nudge) occupies the front passenger seat, turns to me with a suggestion. She thinks it would be a good idea to stop at the hospital to check on the condition of young Mercer.

I'm not so sure. We're not relatives. The hospital staff is not about to release information to just anybody walking in off the street. She looks at me like I don't quite get it.

Right. She's not just anyone. And she has the ID to prove it. Something apparently is telling her that the situation needs her follow-up. Something is nagging at her investigative mind.

As it should be mine, I suddenly conclude. 'A brief stop, folks,' I call behind me, and explain the situation as we make the quick detour needed to get there. 'It should only take Ailsa and me a few minutes. There's a McDonald's across the street. I hear their coffee is better than you might expect. And look at that, a Tim Hortons next to it.' We're back in civilization.

It jerks Alistair out of hibernation. By the look of it, they could all use the java boost. I'll text them when we're done, and show up for a round of caffeine myself before we hit the road again for the two hours it will take to get to St. John's.

Try as they might to look welcoming, hospitals never do. They put me on edge—I've spent too much time within their confines, for broken bones of one variety or another. Given this is what you might call a courtesy visit, I manage to put a lid on the stress level.

Until we get within a few metres of the front entrance. Out through the door comes Donna, wearing an N95. She unhooks it from one ear and lets it dangle from the other.

We keep social distance, a particularly good thing, given her sputtering outburst. 'You heard! Dear God, can you believe it!'

'What happened?'

'What do you mean "what happened?" He's dead! The poor bugger's dead!'

'When?' Ailsa is matter-of-fact, her emotionless police demeanour in play.

'Seven in the morning they called me. By the time I got here he was in the morgue. He didn't last the night.' She put a hand to her mouth. 'Dear God . . .'

'I'm so sorry.' The best I can do.

Ailsa remains pragmatic. 'Have they determined the cause of death?'

'Nobody's saying anything.' She looks at Ailsa, expecting her to have experience in such a situation. But can't resist adding, 'Wouldn't be surprised if they haven't got a bloody clue. They're waiting on an autopsy.'

'The body is on its way into St. John's?'

'Left a half-hour ago.'

That changes the game plan. No point setting foot in the hospital. Inspector Bowmore will be on it as soon as we arrive in the city. The ink won't be dry on the autopsy report before she'll have access to it.

'You've spoken to the local detachment?' Ailsa says.

By which she means the Clarenville RCMP, its red detachment building a few kilometres away. (Along the Trans-Canada, an eager pack of police cars always clustered outside—a fact quickly embedded in the mind of every driver that knows that stretch of highway. An office building that doubles as a speed bump.)

'They took a statement.' I imagine it was a bit of melodrama from behind an N95. 'Not that I could tell them much,' she says. 'Who knows what the frig Lyle got up to. You know actors.'

Right. I still take it with a grain of salt. Donna's been around actors for thirty years. Her sensors are fine-tuned.

I suspect what she has learned is not to volunteer information as far as the police and her summer gang of actors are concerned. Leave well enough alone. I'd say the legalization of pot in Canada took a particularly big load off her mind.

We must part company. Donna faces the unenviable task of relaying the news to the rest of the cast and crew. If ever she needed a supportive embrace, now would be the time.

It's not to be. 'Dear God,' she says, vehemently unhooking the band of elastic from her other ear, shaking her head within what I judge to be exactly two metres of us, then striding off in the direction of her 4Runner.

I glance at Ailsa. She raises her eyebrows. I for one am in need of something more than Tim Hortons. Coffee with one cream, one Splenda, and a sour cream glazed will do nothing to offset the jolt of reality we've just experienced. Ailsa feels the same. I text the others and get them to return to the van. I've heard of a local coffee shop with a solid reputation for cappuccino.

And extraordinary whole-wheat blueberry bread pudding swimming in white chocolate sauce. Under normal circumstances such an offering at Bare Mountain Coffee House, with its bank of windows overlooking the waters of North West Arm, would make for a calming respite.

It does, but only for the time being. Ailsa and I agreed beforehand that we'd save the lump of bad news until after dessert. 'Dead! Really, dead?' Beyond that Alistair is struck dumb. He's suddenly lost all interest in the pool of sauce that remains on his plate.

The others are equally stupefied. 'Maybe it was anaphylactic shock after all,' Jillian offers timidly.

'Totally unnerving for Rising Tide,' says Jeremy. 'Donna must be devastated.'

An understatement, I assure them. That being said, our minds are fixed on the death of the young man and how it could possibly have happened.

We remain in the dark, for now. There is nothing to be done except reboard the van and head for St. John's. We drive in silence. The time for speculation is past. We leave the cause of death to science.

Death, unexplained or otherwise, is not a note on which I ever want a tour to end. We'll try to move on with our lives, thankful that we at least are able to do that.

SCENE 5

THERE IS A long exhale once a tour is complete. Everyone has returned safely home and you, tour guide, are no longer responsible for anyone's level of satisfaction with the world. You breathe easily once again, recall the highlights, count the cash, and kick back in anticipation of the arrival of your charmer of a son and nonconformist of a dog.

The leftover Peat Monster is hardly in the glass when they burst in. Gaffer, lead and harness still attached, leaps onto my lap and flashes his tongue in the direction of my face. I love that about a dog. He craves his master, no matter how good he's had it in my absence.

'Nick, pal, how did it go?' The dog gives way so I can get to my feet and give my son a hug.

'Good,' he says. Always a relief.

'No disasters?'

'Nothing major. You know. The usual. Mom wasn't keen when he crapped in her periwinkle, but, you know, that's par for the course. Otherwise, all good. No throw-ups. No diarrhea. No infections.'

'There we go. All's well that ends well.'

'How about you?'

'Didn't end so well.' I relate the theatre incident. 'These things happen. Anaphylactic shock is my educated guess. To be honest, I'm just glad to be out of the picture. Have some time to unwind.'

'Order in Indian food, have a beer, switch to Laphroaig, reread Hemingway, and fall asleep in the comfy chair.'

He knows me well, and pronounces Laphroaig perfectly. His Bruichladdich will need a little work.

We share in the lamb jalfrezi and naan bread. Nick loves it as much as I do, despite the fact it's on the spicy side. The kid is good with spice.

'I wouldn't mind a bit of your beer,' he says, 'to cool down my mouth.'

I frown at him. I'm thinking not.

Another instance of tricky parenting, as if there haven't been enough of them already. This debate has been acting out in my head for a while. Do I let the kid have a little wine or beer with a meal, so it's not such a big deal, so he won't see it as forbidden fruit and go crazy when he does turn legal?

Keeping in mind I'm only half the picture. I can't be allowing it at my place and hoping he doesn't let it slip with his mother. Or, for that matter, the cop who shares their living space. Samantha would likely blow a gasket.

Nick will soon be fifteen. Sounds very far from legal. Sounds as if it shouldn't even be a matter of debate.

'I'm thinking you're a bit young.'

He doesn't argue. Merely testing the waters. That's good.

He waits, then adds. 'Can't be that bad for you. No worse than whisky I bet.'

I let it go.

'Just sayin'.' He grins and goes back to his lamb jalfrezi.

Which can be interpreted in any number of ways. A comment on my drinking habits? He's never seen me drunk, and in any case, rare is the time it's happened once I was out of the singles circuit. Or, for that matter, since I've rejoined it.

Parent by example, as they say. Let the kid see that alcohol can be enjoyed without getting drunk. Like it, but don't crave it. I know when I've had enough. I can go without it, if there's a need. Right now, there's no need.

Nick is out the door with a hug, having explained to Gaffer he'll be back in a couple of days for the weekend. Gaffer, for his part, is happy enough to be back in his regular digs.

There's me and the Laphroaig, which is not going down quite so smoothly as I anticipated. And Netflix, rather than a book. Regardless, I nod off in the comfy chair.

My cell rings. It's in my pocket, and blurry-eyed, I manage to get to it before it goes to message. Unknown number.

'Hope I didn't wake you.' It's Ailsa.

My phone says 10:35. I chuckle in my own defence. 'You know me. Bit early to call it a night.'

'Maybe I should have waited until morning. I thought you would appreciate knowing sooner rather than later.'

Not quite a personal call. Sounding more like an inspector call.

'I've seen the autopsy report.'

I sense hesitation. I sense she might also be saying that she's stepping outside standard procedure by telling me anything. Likely more comfortable doing it in her off-hours rather than at her RCMP desk in the morning.

Really? I'm not your Joe Blow off the street. I wait her out. Let our relationship work its way past police protocol.

'This is strictly confidential of course.'

No need for the "of course."

'There's reason to believe it was something other than an asthma attack.'

Am I surprised? No. Is there any need for the hesitation?

No.

'Anaphylactic shock.' Just as I predicted.

'They've ruled that out completely.'

Really? Okay, I am surprised. It was a near miss, I suspect.

Back to hesitating. She's expecting me to guess again?

'They're waiting on the toxicology report.'

Meaning? 'A formality, I assume.'

'Poison of some kind.'

'Shit.' As in really? Not something I expected.

'He showed signs consistent with ingesting something that eventually killed him.'

'You mean he overdosed?'

'Possibly.'

'Shit.' Poor bastard. 'I mean why would he want to kill himself?'

'Or why would someone want to kill him?'

Standard procedure just went AWOL.

Leaving me the one floundering for words.

'You mean murder?' Trying not to sound like it hasn't entered my head.

'Or he swallowed something unintentionally. Or breathed it in. As I said, they're waiting on the toxicology report.'

There's nothing more to be said. It's obvious she doesn't want to be fanning speculation that what we encountered in Trinity was a crime scene. She's trained to deal in facts, and any action regarding possible criminal intent remains on hold.

Or so she's leading me to believe. I can't think her mind is not swirling with possibilities. Just like mine is.

'I should be going.' A pause, and a tepidly personal 'good night.'

'I'll talk to you tomorrow.'

That's left without comment. 'Sleep well.'

Sleep is not as likely as it was, but that remains unvoiced.

'Cheers.' Likely inappropriate, but ending on a positive note is good, reminiscent of the day only just passed.

Okay, so talk about a jolt to the status quo. We need the results from the toxicology report before ramping up an investigation. I say "we", because, inconvenient or not for the RCMP, if by chance there's murder in the mix then I'm in with both feet, given that I was on the scene at the time, given that I'm a certified private investigator with a complex murder case under my belt. As Ailsa well knows.

Not to sound entitled, but my involvement is obvious. This mind is already scanning the scene backstage for evidence.

I can't be jumping the gun. But it's only professional procedure to lay out a tentative road map, should murder indeed become the operative term, in which case I would be ahead of the game, geared up and able to vault past the preliminaries and step directly into the action.

It is not as if there are constraints on my time. The rest of tour season is dead in the water until tourists from outside the Atlantic Bubble are allowed in. Which is not about to happen this year. COVID case closed.

Sleep is sparse, but morning arrives on time and an anxious day looms. Gaffer, perceptive dog that he is, senses my restrained eagerness. Like the mutt, I could do with extra morning exercise to offset the prolonged anticipation.

Gaffer is not much of a sidewalk dog. He likes his space and I'm thinking unfamiliar parkland would be a good choice, a distraction for both of us. I'm thinking cellphone at hand through a few kilometres of open trail, with side path options to avoid the bane of his existence (other dogs).

After a fifteen-minute drive across town we pull into the main parking lot of Bowring Park. 'Your lucky day, Gaff my lad.'

It being a weekday morning, there are few vehicles. A thinly populated park means less chance of a muzzle-to-muzzle encounter, and less chance of an ensuing barkfest. All good. Positive vibes all around.

Bear in mind a dog walk with Gaffer is an extended sniff session. Unfamiliar territory only prolongs it. I have learned to be patient. I have come to the realization that it's the sensory equivalent of a ravenous human walking into the kitchen of a Michelin three-star.

The lad needs his time to commune with an abundance of nature. In an ideal world I'd let him off-leash so he could have his fill unrestrained, but breaking the park rules would not be wise, given that other canines sometimes lurk in the most unexpected places.

So it's a slow, contemplative sojourn. Gaffer led by his nose, being routed through sections of the park his owner most wants to revisit. Bowring Park is the city's jewel of green space, designed and first opened just prior to WWI, subsequently expanded to its present two hundred acres. There were two statues erected to commemorate the war and it's at these I like to stop and spend some time.

And at the statue of Peter Pan near the Duck Pond, one of only a few cast from the Frampton original in London. It's the statue Gaffer favours. As do children of course, which proves a nuisance since Gaffer has a special fondness for the younger set. My task becomes holding at bay his affectionate urges. Fortunately there are only a few preschoolers, and their attention turns to the live ducks and swans, away from the bronze boy who could fly but never grow up.

Gaffer has interest in the statue for other reasons. A quick tug leads him to a more discreet location, one of the numerous trees of sufficient girth to accommodate a raised hind leg. Gaffer is not impressed but in the end does his business. Then, as if to make a point, he decides to do a second business. Fortunately, before leaving for the walk, I pocketed a thicker than regular, eco-friendly, biodegradable poop bag that brings that extra measure of civic pride to retrieving dog crap.

Tying off the bag is a momentary distraction. I fail to see the black standard poodle entering the scene from the rear. Gaffer does, and lunges in the interloper's direction, jerking his lead out of my hand in the process.

There is something about standard poodles that drives him particularly crazy. Perhaps an inferiority complex, given that he's half miniature poodle himself. Perhaps it's their purebred strut, as if they own the dog world. Whatever the reason, Gaffer lays into the mutt, intelligently keeping enough distance that he's not physically engaging with a fellow canine roughly four times his size. The barking, however, is wild and uncontrolled.

I drop the bag and run to retrieve the lead, cursing under my breath.

The poodle's owner, straining to keep his over-groomed beast from out-and-out retaliation, is not impressed.

'Control your bloody dog if you don't mind.'

The stench of superior dog owner is suffocating.

In short order I have Gaffer off the ground, in my arms, with one hand locked around his jaws to quell the barking.

'Sorry about that.' I'm not above acknowledging when I'm at fault.

The average dog owner would stop at this point, realizing that these things happen, and move on. Not so this twit.

'You know what they say: like owner, like dog,' he gnarls at me, before pulling the swaggering pedigree in the direction of the Duck Pond.

'Really,' I call after him. 'I did notice your mutt has a snotty attitude. You both could do with some training.'

The twit turns and glares, before walking on with his dog, a raised middle finger behind his back. 'Come on, Voltaire.'

Voltaire. He named his dog Voltaire. Good God. Not an ounce more affirmation do I need.

I retrieve the fallen poop bag and keep moving, back in the direction of the parking lot. If Gaffer had it in him to strut, I would definitely encourage it. He doesn't. He'd rather nonchalantly sniff his way homeward, a commoner among canines. I love this dog.

The romp in the park has completed my morning. My afternoon begins in earnest with some intense note-taking. My intention is to record every impression I had of the theatre event in Trinity, from the moment of arrival at the theatre to our departure. Whether it appeared, at this point, significant or insignificant. Everything. As I recall from Unit 3 of my PI training manual, the support of a well-organized, detailed record of a crime scene (potential at this point) is of paramount importance. Memory is imperfect and the longer the gap between actual contact and note-taking, the less detail one is likely to retrieve. The three-page entry is the first in a computer file I have tentatively named "Trinity—the Groundwork".

It cuts well into the afternoon. By the third page the stress of not knowing the results of the toxicology report is beginning to play havoc with my keyboarding skills. Autocorrect is having a field day.

It's time to phone Inspector Bowmore. Not sure it is the best decision, but I run it by Gaffer and he seems good with the idea.

Instead of her cell, I decide to keep it professional and direct the call through her office. I take an affirming breath. 'Hi, it's Sebastian.'

'All good?'

I save the dog-owner story for another time. 'You know, in standby mode.'

'I understand.' Not the response I'd been hoping for.

Then let's get to the point. 'Any word on the toxicology report?'

'Not yet.'

The two-word responses are wearing thin. I deserve more. Our mutual display of affection seems well in the past. I should have taken notes to verify that it actually happened.

'When are you expecting it?'

'These things take time.'

The word count doubled. Progress.

'Lab work is slow-going. Not like in the cop shows. I'd say tomorrow at the earliest.'

There's no confirmation that she'll relay the results once the report does get to her. No confirmation that I will be updated given that we stood shoulder to shoulder at the event under examination.

Let's not let this evolve into a game of cat and mouse. Let's be professional here.

'I'll be waiting to hear from you.' And let's be clear on exactly what should be coming my way. 'I'm looking forward to what the lab has to say.'

'We'll see.'

Meaning *yes, we'll see together what shows up.* Or *yes, I haven't yet made up my mind what I'm willing to share with you.*

'Good-bye. For now.' I can sound equally curt when there's a need.

'Right on.' Her end of the call terminates.

Right on? Bit colloquial for an inspector. There's hope yet.

I realize I've put her in an awkward position. There it is. She's been at this business long enough to realize no investigation runs according to the book. The only constant is the end game. Get on it early, dig deep, use each and every force at your disposal. And yes, Inspector, I like being thought of as a force to be reckoned with.

Twenty-three hours pass, in the words of a great-uncle, as slow as cold molasses running uphill. In times of uncertainty I call upon my ancestors for their pithy expressions. Uncle Boyce knew a lot about relaxing. He lived to be 96.

Gaffer senses the torment of inaction. He encourages me to play catch with him. He is more than willing to chase whatever I throw. Sorry, pal, diversionary tactics are not in the cards.

At 3:06 she calls. My faith somewhat restored.

A single opening pronouncement. 'Confirmed.'

Details would seem to require encouragement. 'So he was poisoned. Not suicide I take it.'

There is hesitation, but she cuts it short. 'Inhaling hydrogen cyanide is not usually intentional, no.'

Hydrogen cyanide. Might sound like sarcasm. But I'm sure it's not.

'Hydrogen cyanide. Really?' It must be obvious I'm in need of additional info.

'Are you familiar with myclobutanil?'

I'm familiar with a lot of things, but I can't say that's among them. 'Not really.'

'I wasn't either.'

Suddenly we're on common ground again.

'A fungicide used to prevent powdery mildew, mostly used by grape growers. Stiffly regulated, but banned altogether in growing cannabis.'

'I see.' Meaning I need more.

'When myclobutanil is heated it changes to hydrogen cyanide.'

The light finally goes on. 'So pot plus myclobutanil is lethal once the joint is lit.'

'If the concentration is high enough.'

'As it was in this case.' Not to put words in her mouth.

'Apparently so. Especially since the victim had a preexisting condition.'

Cyanide poisoning is notorious, of course. Nazi camps. Jonestown massacre. Himmler, Göring, Eva Braun. Rasputin— in that case a failed attempt. An ex–history teacher's list could go on and on.

'The lab is doing further tests,' she adds.

'Which takes time.' But which leads to new, unbroached territory. 'Nevertheless the RCMP is acting on the assumption they have enough to open a murder investigation?'

Eventually there's a 'Yes.'

'The Bonavista RCMP, I'm assuming. And yourself of course, since you were there.'

Silence. God, it's like pulling teeth.

'We need to have a talk.'

I won't say I'm surprised. I will say I'm disappointed. She feels the need for boundaries to be established.

'Can you come by the office?'

I see no reason to delay the inevitable. 'When?'

'Now is good.'

Efficient, as I said. She knows where I live. She knows I could be there in twenty minutes.

'No problem.' Sounding equally on top of the situation. No reluctance. No nonsense.

'See you soon.'

'Good.'

The RCMP Divisional Headquarters is located in the east end of the city in an area known as the White Hills. An impressive building, as federal-government-funded buildings generally are. Whenever I go in one I'm reminded of the worn-out schools I've known, buildings that went decades without being replaced. Thoughts to temper the glow as I'm routed through elaborate security and enter the light-filled atrium.

Ailsa has let it be known I'm expected. I'm directed to her

office, where the uniformed officer is seated behind her desk.

There's much to take in otherwise. Her office has a fine view over the city, indication of her stature within the force. It's increasingly obvious she didn't get to the position she's in by being anything but very good at her job.

Yes, I'm slightly intimidated. And yes, it's something I can set aside and put in a context that reaffirms my own attributes. I smile, knowing that job experience is worth ignoring at times like these.

'This area of the city has quite a lot of history behind it. It was used as military training grounds for both world wars.'

'Yes, I know that.'

'Then you'd know it was under lease to the US Army, and when they pulled out in the early 60s, they dug a huge hole and dumped it full of old trucks, jeeps, oil drums, any crap they didn't want to lug back to the States.'

'There's a file on that in our library.'

'Then you know about the contamination. I'm willing to bet that what you don't know is that what's left of the metal net that was strung across The Narrows during World War II to prevent U-boats entering the harbour is piled up and rusting in the woods not far from this very building.'

'I'm impressed.' And so she should be. '*That* I wasn't aware of.'

As opposed to a lot she is. Like more about the autopsy report that she hasn't told me.

'There are a few things we need to discuss,' she says. Gently turning my attention to the real point of me sitting uncomfortably across from her.

'I agree.'

'As a police officer I have to deal with certain protocols. As you no doubt know. You are considered a member of the general public and unless there is reason to believe that releasing confidential information to you will further an investigation then I'm afraid you'll have to rely on official police press releases.'

Must we sound so formal. Ailsa. It is Ailsa, is it not? We're well past the Inspector Bowmore business, or my memory is playing tricks on me.

If there is any consolation, it is in the fact the officer is as uncomfortable as I am.

This is where I make a stand. I've anticipated this scenario unfolding, if not quite so stiffly.

'Is my plan to further the investigation? Absolutely. Will I pick up the trail where we left it in Trinity? Absolutely. And who will be the first to know what I uncover? The RCMP.'

'That's what I was afraid of.'

'Afraid? There's nothing to be afraid of, Ailsa.'

'Sebastian, listen to me.'

This is the point at which any pretense of a personal bond plummets from view.

I fight against it. 'Fire away, Ailsa.' I force a smile.

'Sebastian, let's be frank.'

Why not. What else have I got to lose.

'You're overstepping the boundaries. You can't be interfering in an RCMP investigation.'

'Interfering?' Not good, by me. Now who's overstepping a boundary?

'Maybe not intentionally interfering.'

Forget the "intentionally". I wouldn't be interfering. Period.

I try to be tactful. I ignore the uniform and assume I can reach her on a plain, factual level. 'As a licensed private investigator I have the right to pursue an enquiry within the parameters of the law.'

'I realize that. What I'm saying is we have a job to do and a separate, parallel investigation might only confuse the landscape.'

Interesting way of putting it. She's being very careful.

Which leads me to thinking there are other factors at play here. Like the inexperience of the cops at the detachment in Bonavista. Like the fact that murder investigation is something that rarely comes their way. Their need for an open playing field, under Inspector Bowmore's direction.

'In that case, we work together. We keep our distance, but keep each other informed. Surely you're not opposed to that on principle. A second set of professional eyes is always useful. You have only so much time to devote to this case. Private investigators are less visible. We don't attract attention. We can go down paths your uniforms might not be able to go.'

I know and she knows cops and PIs often work together. Suddenly it strikes me that she might be questioning my competence. Jesus. If that's what it is then we do have an issue. A very big issue.

'Okay.' A tentative step toward my perspective? 'Okay.'

The second okay, resigned. An okay that points to the notion she's going against her better judgment.

I'll live with that. I'll give her the time she needs to come around to seeing just how valuable I can be.

'We can't hire you.'

I don't think it's a joke. Whatever it is, it never crossed my mind.

Not that Inspector Bowmore needs to know that. 'That's too bad, but there it is. I'm good.'

I leave the office, relieved more than anything. We dodged our respective bullets.

I'd foreseen the wreck of a relationship, but as things now stand we're smiling and civil and I, at least, am confident that we will be able to reshape the intact pieces into something professional and mutually respectful.

Not exactly romantic, I know. But there it is. Okay. At this point.

The security guard is pleased to see me. Another safely executed entry and exit. 'You have a good day, my friend,' I tell him. 'Take a break. Get outside. Enjoy the view.' I like it when I leave a cop station feeling positive. It hasn't always been the case.

There's a certain power vibe in the air when you have a confluence of cops, the understanding they're in control of any and all situations, that out of judicial obligation they listen to what you have to say, but ultimately they make decisions and you learn to live with them.

A show of humour is not normally part of the mix. It complicates matters.

Okay, time to move on.

Let's have a little single malt and strategize. I quickly conclude that drinking Scotch and sitting in the comfy chair in the capital city is not where I need to be. The investigative focus is Trinity and the sooner I get back to the scene of the crime the better. The criminal trail runs cold only too quickly.

Which raises another detail that, regrettably, has to be faced. The state of my finances. Until the tour business picks up, the cash flow remains in a state of flux. There is the option of rerouting attention to other work (insurance fraud, spousal infidelity, debtor tracing), but that all seems so paltry at the moment, what with the whiff of murder in the air.

Which means taking a bite out of savings until life returns to normal and my bread-and-butter mainland tourists are again able to sign up. Not something I want to be doing, but mutual funds have rebounded, which gives me a little leeway.

Still, travel on the cheap is the preferred option. I'm some-one who can do without starred accommodation and an ocean view. I can eat on the cheap, too, and feel no pain. A boiled egg and toast for breakfast, soup and chicken wrap for lunch. As long as there's Scotch by the firepit at night.

'What's for supper?'

Nick has a way of entering the picture at the most opportune moment. His arrival, full backpack slung off the shoulder, means it's the Friday night of his weekend with his faithful dog and father. Something to celebrate. With food, as expected.

'What say we order in?' he says, romping on the carpet with the eager Gaffer.

'What say we check the fridge first?'

Let frugality take hold. I need the practice.

The refrigerator reveals frozen chicken breasts, a single red pepper, celery, broccoli (yellowing but redeemable) and an ambitious knob of fresh ginger.

'Stir-fry—again?' says Nick.

'Let's not jump to conclusions.' I head to my laptop. 'O, ye of little faith.'

He invariably rolls his eyes at that handy rebuke.

One of the great joys of the web is its talent for coming up with recipes when you punch in the ingredients available in a sparsely stocked fridge. I endure three screens of stir-fries to find it, but when I do it practically glows: *Ricardo's Chicken Curry with Red Pepper and Coconut Milk.*

I scan the ingredients. 'Check, check, check,' on the spices. 'And as for the coconut milk?' A quick trip to the larder and there it sits in anticipation of finally being called upon to perform. And rice. Good to go on the rice. 'Wicked. Let the culinary adventure begin!'

Nick shakes his head and chuckles. 'Don the apron! Unsheath the knife!' He savours the theatrics.

'You're on veg detail. I'll have a go at the clucker meat.'

Forty-five minutes later, the performance over, we sit at the kitchen table and dig in.

'No beer tonight?'

I've been waiting for that. Spice and beer have been my

habitual pairing. 'Cutting back. I'm feeling a few pounds heavier after the last tour. Wouldn't want Doctor Frank on my case again.'

'I'd switch to light beer if I were you.' He smiles broadly.

'Cute, Nick.'

He knows how much I detest light beer. I have been known to call it cat piss. Likely in front of him.

'I'll nip that one in the Bud Light.' Thumbs-up for Dad.

He's itching for a smarter comeback. The point was to jettison the beer talk with the underage son.

'I'm heading back to Trinity on Monday.' And jettison it decisively. 'By the look of it we have murder on our hands.'

The kid's eyes immediately ignite.

His pivotal role in the case last year of a naked young man strangled and left half-buried under rock, undoubtedly, comes quickly to mind.

'Poisoned.' Murder, but much less gruesome.

I had planned to ease into telling him, but no need to put it off. I take to the comfy chair and enjoy a small, post-meal dram without any further adolescent analysis of my drinking habits.

I lay out the possible scenarios and swear him to secrecy. Which is nothing less than a direct shot of adrenalin for the teenage mind.

'Wow.' He blows out a puff of air that radiates enthusiasm.

'It's wide open at the moment as to who might have done it and why.'

'Can I come?'

'Come where?'

'To Trinity, with you.'

'Sorry, pal, not a good idea.'

'Ah, c'mon.' With that crooked grin, like what he's hearing is ridiculous.

'No way.'

If pleading goes nowhere, try another tactic. 'What are you going to do with Gaffer? Mom won't have him back again so soon, I'll tell you that right now.'

'I might just take him with me.' Which, to be honest, only just emerged as a possibility. 'Or Jeremy might take him.' I'm suddenly thinking that might be a harder sell than it used to be. Not sure what Adam thinks of dogs.

'You can't possibly do your work with him in tow. I'll look after him while you're busy poking around.'

'Poking around?'

'Where you staying?'

'Which kills your suggestion altogether. I expect I'll be camping. To save money.'

'Camping? I love camping.'

'Think of it. Two people and a dog in a pup tent. Not going to happen.'

'It's a two-person pup tent!' Somehow he remembers it from the only time he and his parents ever went camping, when he was about five. An unmitigated disaster. He remembers because, prior to going, his mother and I had a protracted discussion on the size of tent to buy. In the interest of economy, I won out. The start of the aforementioned unmitigated disaster.

My head is still shaking, no.

'Tell you what,' he says, as if there's a deal to be made. 'I'll do all the cooking. That way you'll have even more time to poke around.'

'First of all, a PI doesn't "poke around", as you call it. He plans ahead, makes enquiries, records observations, uncovers leads . . .'

'Absolutely. You're professional. For a second I forgot you finished in the 90th percentile on the final exam.'

Flattery and/or sarcasm will get him nowhere.

'But *you're* forgetting one important detail,' he says.

'And what might that be?' How deep will he dig this time?

'As I recall from the custody agreement, I'm due another week of summer vacation with you. When are you going to fit that in? Time is running out. Didn't you hear—it's back to in-school classes starting the day after Labour Day.' He checks his phone. 'Which, according to my calculation, is fourteen days from Tuesday.'

Contrary to his calculation, I have not forgotten. 'We'll fit it in when I get back.'

'Hope you don't uncover too much and have to cut short your time on the case so you and me can take in several very loud movies. Or a few afternoons at the games arcade in the mall.'

Smartass.

'Take me to Trinity and you'll kill two birds with one stone.'

Holding firm. I will admit that me on my own with Gaffer in Trinity is not an option. He'd forever be in the way of getting anything done. If Jeremy plus Adam won't take him, then I can always put him in a kennel.

'And you know Gaffer hates kennels.'

Mind-reader/smartass.

Let's put it this way. Life is too short not to give in and let the son get his way when the situation warrants. I can be the bigger man. Besides, he's hasn't been outside the city all summer. He could do with roughing it in the outdoors.

To his credit, he knows better than to gloat. He smiles tentatively and goes about cleaning up from supper while I sip some peat, undisturbed.

There's a lot to be said for father, son, and dog in a pup tent. Without Wi-Fi. Except with roaming charges. Which is not going to happen.

That little tidbit I will refrain from mentioning until we get there. Any bets he'll be singing a different tune? I chuckle to myself as I take another refreshing sip of peat.

The next day, I run the trip past Samantha. I decide it best not to mention Trinity specifically, in case she somehow got wind of what went on there, via the cop in her life. Protracted pillow talk.

'The Bonavista Peninsula, again?'

'I'm looking to polish next year's tour.'

She's only a little pissed. 'I wish you had let me know. I would have made plans.'

A romantic little getaway with the good Inspector Olsen? 'Spur of the moment is always exciting.'

A lead balloon of course. 'You're always so pragmatic,' she says. The sarcasm drips.

If the truth be told she warms rather quickly to the notion of as much as two weeks without Nick. No bored teenager needing attention. It frees her up to do just what she wants when she wants. Kick back and relax before school starts up again and she resumes her workload as principal. Kick back and stoke the fires of romance, if my mind were willing to go there. Play house, uninterrupted.

'Just be careful.' Her final words on the subject. I'd say she's scheduling a trip to La Senza as we speak.

There's no decent reason for my mind to bend in that direction. I have a pup tent to dig out from the bowels of the storage room, sleeping bags to air out, a grocery list to fill. And a trip to Lester Lube, for the only oil change in my foreseeable future.

It could be worse. I could have COVID and be running out of Scotch.

Nick finishes up in the kitchen and stands near me, mutt in his arms. 'Whataya at?' he says. Bright and chipper.

'Trying to decide whether to buy canned beans.'

'I love canned beans.'

Since when?

'And how about Vienna sausages? I'd say at least a dozen cans.'

Gotta love it. Gotta love the notion of sitting around a campfire, peeling back the lid on the Maple Leaf little blue tin. Vienna sausages. The name alone is inspiring. Takes me back to my youth. I gorged on more than a few cans of the godawful little wieners around campfires with the b'ys. I even learned the trick of getting the middle wiener to pop up without having to destroy it in the process of extracting it with a fork. It's a manly piece of culinary info that I'll have to pass on to my son at the appropriate moment.

By the time Monday morning rolls around, the trunk is packed with what I consider "the essentials". (That would be no to the hammock and no to the dog bed.) Even at that there's a sizable overflow into the back seat. (In my wisdom yesterday I drew an indelible line at the battery-operated, extendable, rotating marshmallow roasting sticks that Nick saw advertised in a Walmart flyer.) Whatever we don't have we do without. The quintessential adage when we're an hour past the time we said we'd leave.

Four hours, ten minutes later we're ensconced at a campsite in Lockston Path Provincial Park. Sun out, tent up, food on the picnic table, bug spray applied, Gaffer finished barking at some brazen squirrel. Does the camping life get any better than this?

'What do you mean there's no Wi-Fi?'

ACT TWO

SCENE 1

IF THERE IS one thing I learned from my PI training it's to approach any case with backbone, limited though resources might be. True, I lack the high-tech gadgetry that soaks up bank accounts and leaves guys wasting their time getting it to work. I place my bets where they belong: on a natural aptitude to engage with people, and what I consider an innate ability to uncover the scattered pieces of a criminal puzzle and gradually, thoughtfully, reposition each of them until they form a complete picture.

I don't carry a weapon. Other than two fists of dubious impact. Guns in the hands of Canadian PIs are prohibited by law. And let's face it, Newfoundland is not the Bronx. Or even Toronto. Not even the Hawaii of my TV-watching youth. I'm not your Magnum, PI. Might have once imagined I looked like Tom Selleck, but I never did.

No, it's me, not a weapon, that does the talking. And that, my friend, is an unqualified strength.

I have to say that in Donna Butt I've met my match.

I might even say I pale in comparison. The Artistic Director of Rising Tide Theatre is never at a loss for words. It is one of the things I've come to love about her. She can poke fun at anybody, but just as easily laugh at herself, always an admirable trait. Then, in the same breath, turn deadly serious.

The trick is catching her at the right time. If she's got something else that needs her attention, forget it. Take your ball and go home.

Reading her mood is the other half of the battle. And once you've mastered both bits, there's no end to the indelible exchanges that could come your way. I'm back in Trinity to get in on the game, not sit on the sidelines. I need Donna to sign me up. Nothing is going to happen without her nod of approval.

I play it low-key, leave it to her to make the first move. I collect two tickets and Nick and I slip into *Shenanigans* without her noticing.

Just prior to the start she again stands before her audience. She's far from the woman I met a few days before. She still has the plastic shield, but the face behind it is distressed and gravely serious.

She relates the episode that befell the cast the last time they took to the stage. Lyle Mercer collapsed in the middle of a skit and died in hospital the following day. She dedicates this performance to Lyle, 'a dear, sweet man, friend to all who knew him.'

The latter is not quite true, of course. He had at least one enemy. That, she doesn't mention.

The fact that Lyle Mercer was murdered is best left unsaid. No theatregoers would enjoy the show if they had murder on their minds. As Donna departs, one hand under the shield wiping away tears, she catches sight of me. There's a double take, then a quick nod. I interpret it as confirmation she'll see me after the show.

The cast does its level best, all things considered. And, in any case, the rest of the audience sits oblivious to that extra zip of energy they brought to it before Lyle's untimely demise. His replacement, when I study him closely, looks to be one of the fellows I saw working backstage on the night it all happened. He's far from a convincing Solomon Noddy.

Nevertheless, a Newfoundland audience prefers to be generous. When the show is over, the cast gets a solid round of applause and the folks file out feeling they got their money's worth. Nick's citified teenage mind liked it well enough, at least what he saw of it, what with two trips to the car to check on Gaffer. As the audience continues to depart, I wait on the wharf that adjoins the theatre, on a bench, looking across the moon-brightened waters to the lights of Trinity East. Nick is off walking Gaffer.

Donna emerges eventually, locking the main door of the theatre before catching sight of me. It's hard to judge her mood in the semi-darkness.

'Whataya doing here?' she asks, maintaining the gap between us.

Not unkind, just straight to the point. 'Thought I'd bring the young fellow out to see the show.'

'I saw him flittin' back and forth. Short attention span?'

I mutter something about a dog in a car, but there's not much point. She has a lot more on her mind.

'What did you think of the show?'

'Pretty good.'

'You're right, it was the shits. All this hit them like a bloody ton of bricks. And now the cops show up and pummel them with questions.'

'It's bound to happen in a murder investigation.'

'Gentle Jesus.'

That pretty well sums up her mood.

She slumps onto the other end of the other bench. 'God knows I've been through a hell of a lot running a theatre company, but murder takes the friggin' cake.'

She could do with an embrace, and, by rights, it should come from someone who knows her better than I do. Compassion has few boundaries in Newfoundland, but in this case social distancing has become one.

I'm virtually wrapping arms around a sea of pent-up emotion. Even from two metres I feel the quiver of her frustration at what has overtaken the remainder of her theatre season. She has less than two weeks to go.

'Hell on bloody wheels,' she says when we regain our poise.

That sums it up from her perspective. Not only is she struggling to complete a season fractured by COVID-19, but she's been forced to come to terms with the fact that out there is a murderer who might be as close as another actor on the very same stage. Live theatre is fraught with uncertainty at the best of times, but this? 'Mother of God, where will it end?'

She's in no state for the talk I need to have with her. 'I'd like to come by in the morning and discuss a few theories about what happened.'

She's tired and frustrated. She looks at me. Add perplexed.

'When I'm not leading tour groups, I'm a private investigator.'

Something else to cramp her mind.

'We'll talk in the morning. I think I can help you get some perspective on all this.'

She peers at me, as if I stepped ashore from another planet.

At this point Nick shows up. Ever-affectionate Gaffer heads straight for the disgruntled Donna. Not a good idea. Fortunately Nick holds him off, nodding in time with my introduction.

Donna perks up, seeing the adolescent dread at being the centre of attention. She starts needling him straight away. 'Your old man got his hands full with you or what?' It's her devilish way of connecting with him.

Nick's not sure what to make of her. He chuckles awkwardly.

'What took you so long?' I ask him.

'On his phone,' Donna says.

She's right of course. No hiding the guilt. 'You can't be using up the data.'

'Never mind your father,' she says to Nick. 'You come by tomorrow and I'll give you our password.'

She's won him over, as quick as that. Friend for life.

He's not met anyone quite like her. This I relish—getting him out of his comfort zone, broadening his view of the world, nudging him into navigating a way through new relationships. As we arrive back at the campground, I'm thinking—all part of the business of fatherhood; right up there with food and shelter.

'Dad, your snoring is keeping me awake.'

Out of his comfort zone in more ways than one. I turn in the sleeping bag, onto my side, barely out of the stupor.

Gaffer yelps. I flick on my cellphone light. Nick's head is buried under his pillow. Gaffer is not quite so dexterous, though I see he is able to curl his tongue into a near-empty bag of Cheezies. I flick off the light, turn over and fall back to sleep.

I let the young fellow and the mutt sleep in. Eventually the smell of bacon frying drags them past the tent flap and into sunlight, both off in search of a place to take a leak.

'This is the life, Nick, my boy!' Deliberately and painfully animated. And with pancakes fried in bacon grease. 'You gotta love it.'

'I know I promised to do the cooking . . .' His defence stifled by a mouthful of food.

'I know, I know, a growing boy needs his rest.'

He swallows in time to make his point. 'You were snoring, and I mean loud.'

The boy exaggerates.

'Must have driven Mom crazy.'

Now then. My mouth tightens.

He has the smarts to know he's stepped into territory that's off limits. He hardly ever mentions his father and mother in the same breath anymore, never when it conjures up an image of both of us anywhere near a bedroom.

'Great breakfast,' he says.

I let it pass.

The rest is silence. Coffee and slightly burnt toast. The truth is my snoring was a sore point during the downturn in the marriage. Maybe deliberate on my part, who knows. In any case I would have thought my recent weight loss might have done something to quell it. Apparently not.

Nick gets dressed and is eager to clean up from breakfast so we can get going. Act of contrition or thirst for Wi-Fi? It doesn't really matter.

Camping makes me feel slightly grubby. I expect that will only intensify as the days wear on, but for the moment at least I remain in the presentable category. Besides, Donna needs to experience me at my casual best. It's a theatre company after all. It's not what you look like, it's how you play your part.

The part I play is someone who might be able to relieve some of the pressure she's feeling right now. Someone with the investigative skill to cast light on answers to the three questions that are informing every move she makes: Who did the job on Lyle? Is that person among the dozen cast and crew still strutting her stage? Will that son-of-a-bitch do it again?

She's receptive. It takes some manoeuvring on my part but I'm making headway.

'You want my permission to poke around, see what you can find out?'

That's basically it. Though I need to frame it somewhat

differently. 'Private investigators have their ways, without being obvious about it.'

'What the hell can you do that the cops can't?' Straight to the point and all of 9:30 in the morning. The coffee and muffin littered over the jumble of paper crowding her laptop seem to fuel the process.

'The second cops show up, alarms go off. They intimidate. Potential informants clam up. Sources dumb down because they don't want to be involved.'

'That's your theory?'

'It's more than a theory, Donna. It's fact.' Firm in my belief she wants decisiveness in her life right now.

More action on her coffee and muffin. I've hardly touched mine. It stands as a measure of my seriousness.

Her mind is driving through the proposition. 'How do you propose to do this? You don't know the cast and crew from a hole in the wall.'

She has a point. But not one to put me off my game. Not one I haven't chewed over several times.

'You pretend you hire me as an office assistant. I quickly ease my way into getting to know them . . .'

'There's no money to hire you. What—free labour? Makes me look bad. Besides, if you find anything, whatever the frig you've been up to is bound to come out.'

'I'll give you a good rate.'

'You're not in the budget. I got funding agencies to answer to. How's that going to look—Rising Tide hires a private eye on taxpayers' money. No way, not going there.'

Her bullheadedness is in full view. I refuse to think we've reached an impasse.

More coffee. The last of the muffin.

'Can you act?' she says.

'Act? Like *act* act?'

'I run a friggin' theatre company. What the frig else do you think I mean?'

Losing patience. Not good.

'High school. Gander.'

She doesn't dismiss it outright. Her hesitation feeding on the fact that my hometown had a reputation as a hotbed of high school drama.

'We took top prize in the Provincials.'

'What play?'

'*A Midsummer Night's Dream.*'

'Really?'

'A condensed version . . . we had it down to forty minutes.'

'Shakespeare would have been thrilled. What role did you play?'

'Puck. And Philostrate. We did a lot of doubling.'

'No doubt.'

All the time she's ruminating. She curls her hair with one finger. Finally, it emerges. 'Solomon Noddy.'

I don't quite get the point.

'Well, what about it? The fellow who took over from Lyle is hopeless. Think you could pull off Solomon Noddy?'

She wants me on stage, acting? In front of an audience. Office assistant sounds much more realistic.

'That way I could legitimately put you on the payroll. You could still fake some office work on the side.'

'Give me time to think about it.'

'There is no time. The next show is in two days.'

Deep, ambivalent breath. 'I could give it a try.'

'There's no giving it a try. Four performances left in the season. Either you're in, or you pack up and go home.'

In that case. I deliver a broad smile. 'Sign me up.'

She digs through a filing cabinet, and lays before me a stapled, coffee-stained pile of pages. She checks the time on her phone. 'You got four hours to learn your lines. Be back here at two. We'll do a run-through.' And, in case I missed the point, 'Next show in two days.'

Her office door opens to a deck outside the theatre. She steps past the door. 'Nick, my love, your father's ready. He'll need help practising his lines.'

Nick meets me at the end of the deck, still managing to text while holding Gaffer's lead. He finally looks up. 'Did she say lines?'

'There's accommodation,' Donna calls, 'if you need it.'

'Did she say accommodation? Like not in a tent?'

'Free of charge. Wi-Fi included,' she adds, before disappearing inside.

'Yes!' That would be Nick.

And yes, she said lines, a batch of them as I recall from the show last night. During the drive back to the campsite I get Nick to scrutinize the script beginning to end, underlining every word uttered by Solomon Noddy. The car parked, Nick sets to work deconstructing the tent and packing up the gear while I sit at the picnic table and bury myself in the script.

One of the tricks to learning lines, as I recall from my Puck/Philostrate days, is to write them out, slowly, deliberately. Not what I expected to be filling pages in my pricey, leather-bound notebook reserved for criminal investigation. Yet, for all my dread at just what the frig I've gotten myself into, there's a bizarre thrill emerging. What bloody lengths a PI will go to to get at the truth! I attack the script with dogged determination to remake myself into the young buck that eagerly took to that high school stage those many years ago. I shed decades.

Lunch preparation is out of the question. I need Nick to run the lines with me. We snack on bananas, mini Babybels, and Vienna sausages. A dubious combo but food is very far from my mind.

The promised demonstration of how to get the little bug-
gers out of the can takes all of a few seconds (flip the lid, drain
the juice, smack the can on the wrist and up pops the middle
weenie). Nick is impressed by my dexterity, not so much by
what's in the can.

No time to be griping about Vienna sausages. I step away
from the picnic table and into open space that I easily imagine
as theatre stage. I nod to Nick. 'Hit me.'

For a first run, it goes well. A little prompting, but that's
par for the course. The second time, much better. By the third
I definitely have the hang of it.

While Nick packs up the car, I retreat to the script for some
fine-tuning.

Two o'clock approaches faster than I would like. I'm not
panicking, but I can't escape some tension. I have a lot riding
on this, and Nick hears it in my voice. 'Dad, man, relax. You
know you know the lines. Let it flow.'

I pull into the parking lot of Rising Tide. Nick and Gaffer
are off for further exploration of the town. I have ten minutes
to work myself into the headspace to pull this off.

I talk myself into it. It's not as if I haven't got a keen memory. Not as if I haven't been mimicking people for years and
getting a good laugh. Not as if I'm scared shitless.

I take a series of stabilizing breaths en route to the entrance
into the theatre. My confidence peaks. I make my way past the
box office, past the double doors, to where Donna and a few
cast members are sitting around a table in front of the stage.

'Here he comes,' she says, 'the man of the hour. Welcome
to the Rising Tide bubble.'

Yes, let everyone's attention focus directly on me. I do away
with the mask. I smile pleasantly and nod to them all as Donna
does the introductions.

'Sebastian is a friend from St. John's. A townie, but we won't hold that against him.' Laughter ensues. But it's not meant to linger. 'Sebastian is a tour guide, but he hit a dry spell this year, as have we all. So he was open to any new gigs to come his way. He hasn't had a lot of acting experience, but what he does have really impressed me. So I said, what the heck, let's give him a shot. With only a few shows left in the season, what have we got to lose.' She draws her hand to her face and sniffs. 'Lyle was a generous person. He would have wanted it this way.'

Donna is an accomplished actor in her own right. A nice encouraging push for them to take me into their confidence.

I'm here to play along. 'I might be a little rusty, but I'll give it my best shot.'

'Well, we're here to scrape off that rust.' Suddenly, all business. 'First we'll do a quick read-through. All set. Here we go.'

The script reading goes extremely well. I slip into Solomon Noddy, a hand in the proverbial glove. She's pleased. I read the other faces. My fellow actors are impressed, relieved even. I take it the previous crewman-cum-actor was more than a little challenging to work with on stage.

'Okay, on your feet everyone.' This rehearsal is an un-scheduled intrusion in her day, so she needs to get it over with and move to other business. In any case, I gather Rising Tide is not known for its extensive rehearsal periods.

Onstage, Solomon Noddy proves a bit more of a challenge.

The other actors walk through their roles, tepidly to say the least. No need, they figure, to go flat out when Donna already knows they can nail their parts in front of an audience. I, on the other hand, am expected to jump headfirst into my part, no holdback, play it like my life depends on it.

I mishandle a few lines. No, actually, I fuck them up.

The others look at Donna like *okay, now what?*

She reins everyone in. 'Let's take it from the top. Boost it up. Except for Sebastian.' She sets her sights on me. 'Slow down. Relax. I know you know the lines. Solomon Noddy is not a complicated man. He has his point of view, which he thinks is right, and he sticks with it. Forget the accent for now. That'll come. You look the part, just ease into it. Remember, nobody's judging you.'

Right. Get me to believe that.

I continue to fuck up, but less frequently with each successive run through. An hour passes and I pretty well have it. As close to down pat as I'm likely to get. For now.

'Good man.' Her final, carefully chosen, curt analysis to end the session.

Before she leaves she draws me aside, together with one of the other actors in the piece. His name is Randy.

Not a name you hear much anymore. For obvious reasons. Make that Randy Dicks. A double whammy.

It is not helped by his noticeably stiff reaction when Donna informs him, 'Sebastian's all set to move in. He and his son. Lots of room.'

Donna would have told him beforehand that we would be his new housemates. She definitely wouldn't have just sprung it on him, making his cool reception even more apparent.

Though not to Donna, who has already given me far more time than she had allotted. She's off, leaving the two of us to sort things out.

'Lots of room,' he says, 'since Lyle is no longer there.'

So that's it. Donna had made no mention of the fact that we're moving in where Lyle had moved out, so to speak. Interesting. A lucky break, I'm thinking. Literally taking over where the deceased left off. And likely a deliberate move on Donna's part. A very clever woman.

For Randy I play the thankful new cast member. Thankful to have a place to stay. Thankful it's a house and not a pup tent.

'Take the first left into Trouty. Go along by the river.

Turquoise house with a yellow door. Can't miss it. Go on in, it's unlocked. Lyle's room is the one with the unmade bed. I left it that way.'

Very hospitable of him. Should I award him Superhost status now or wait until we have a few days under our belts?

A professional smile nonetheless. 'Thanks, Randy. Great.' Dickhead.

That aside, I'm thrilled of course. Not only have I landed in the house where the murder victim resided right up to the time he met his fateful end, but I'll be entrenched with someone who lived and worked with him day in, day out for weeks. Someone who likely has a lot more useful information than he's aware of. Information he is willing to share. Or not, in which case Randy, dickhead, could very quickly turn into Randy, suspect.

I find Nick on the bench outside the theatre. Gaffer has proven to be an attraction for the actors who've just left rehearsal. I might not have been so popular with them, but affable Gaffer has softened the situation.

'Cute dog, Sebastian.'

'Thanks.' I take it as a much-needed commendation.

As they wander off, I slip Gaffer one of the treats I carry in my pocket for emergencies.

'So. How did it go?' says Nick. 'What took so long?'

'Practice makes perfect.' Which proves sufficient to halt the questions.

We head to Trouty, stopping by a convenience store en route to pick up a six-pack, compensation for the sweat of rehearsal, together with a few ingredients for supper.

Trouty is a hamlet about ten minutes south of Trinity and relatively anonymous. Or was, up until 2010. That September Hurricane Igor struck, propelling the community into national headlines.

Full-fledged hurricanes are rare in Newfoundland, and

Category 4 Igor was a brute. It left a swath of destruction that smacked Trouty particularly hard. Fierce wind and soaring water levels, wharves and fishing sheds smashed to pieces, the bridge connecting homes to the rest of the province wiped out. So bad the Canadian military was sent in straight away.

For a while it was a disaster zone. Eventually the waters receded and, with bridge reconstruction underway, the local ladies emerged with mugs of tea and plates of tea buns to soothe the weary soldiers, especially the handsome, brawny young charmers who spoke with such endearing French Canadian accents.

Trouty recovered and went back to its quiet existence. It has a few summer residents, but nothing close to the numbers that show up in Trinity. But then comes the murder of Lyle Mercer, setting Trouty back on its heels once again. And now there's two new lads unpacking a car in front of the house where the victim resided.

Within five minutes an older guy wanders over from across the street. If the monster-size pickup parked in front of his house is any indication, he's far from your typical, well-worn retiree. The way he's dressed only confirms it—Nike track pants, sandals, and yellow polo shirt, its alligator logo in defiance of his extended midsection.

'How ya gettin' on?'

He hasn't lost his accent, however. The opening line is the standard local lubricant to conversation. He's making little effort to hide his curiosity.

'Good, b'y.'

When I find myself in outport Newfoundland the townie in me gives way to sounding like I could be straight from the bay, or at least have lived a few years in one. I introduce myself and Nick, who gathers up another couple of bags from the trunk and heads back in the house, which Gaffer at the moment is scouting out.

'Ig Payne.' He's itching to shake hands, but an exchange of raised palms will have to do.

'Ig?' To be sure I got it right. 'Good to meet ya.'

'My father was a big fan of Sherlock Holmes. You know Arthur Conan Doyle. Ignatius was Doyle's other middle name.' Obviously, the guy has had to explain it more than once.

'Ah.' Ignatius, I'm thinking, one up from Conan.

'Moving in for a while? Working for Donna I take it?'

On a first-name basis with Donna and one step ahead of the game.

He's caught my surprise. 'I rent this place to Rising Tide, for the summers.'

'Ah,' again. In which case he might prove invaluable. 'I'm taking over from Lyle. Very sad what happened. You knew him then?'

'A bit.'

I need more than that. I make a calculated addition, 'Looks like he might have been poisoned.'

'I heard.' But no more.

Worth taking another stab at. 'Must have been a shocker.'

'No doubt about that. I'd see the guy outside on his phone, texting and smoking up. Like I told the cops, he liked his weed.'

I'm thinking there could be a lot more he didn't tell them. 'You talked much to Lyle?'

'The more he smoked, the more he talked. You know.'

Getting there.

'These guys, they show up for a summer, maybe two. Never know what they get up to in their off-time.'

'Any suspicions?'

'I stay clear of it. As long as they don't wreck the place, that's all I care about.'

A dead end, for now. I don't want to be pushing it and

having him think I'm any more than a curious actor settling himself in the house.

'Lots of cops around,' he volunteers. 'Randy is getting fed up with it, but I'd expect more if I were you.'

'Thanks for the heads-up.'

'You've met Randy for sure,' he says. 'Another strange bird. He'll talk to you, but when he does, he's doing you a favour. Weird for a fellow from Lushes Bight. If he was from St. John's, now, I could see it. But not Lushes Bight.'

For someone who seemed reluctant to talk about Lyle, he's got plenty to say about Lyle's housemate.

'Must be love, can't be the weather, as they used to say. The horny acting crowd, you know, they're all looking for their bit for the summer. Randy, I'd say, is still reeling from his good luck.'

Plenty to say and no telling which direction his mind will take.

'*You* haven't got to worry about that,' he throws in, his chuckle followed by a wink and a nod.

No need for the sorry attempt at humour, Ig. Not at your age. Not with that gut.

As I close the trunk of the car, Ig reluctantly moves off. With a final word to the good. 'You like fresh cod?'

All is forgiven. I'm not about to say no to fresh cod.

'Next time I go out in the boat, I'll come by with a few fillets.'

Good on ya, Ig.

Gone then, to whatever untold excitement rural retirees encounter on any given day.

Nick and I and Gaffer take up residence in a three-bedroom bungalow, sparsely furnished, painted a pale, institutional green throughout, and with an ancient refrigerator that hums. Nevertheless, a step up from the pup tent, if somewhat less welcoming.

I start by sweeping the linoleum floor, stacking the empty beer bottles in a corner, and having a go at the pile of encrusted plates and bowls spilling out of the kitchen sink and onto the counter. A good portion of the crust is neon orange, and that can mean only one thing—a hopeless cook selling his soul to Kraft Dinner.

Nick grudgingly puts a dish towel to use while I wash. 'I don't see why we should be . . .'

'A gesture,' I tell him. 'We do the guy a favour. He, in turn, appreciates us being here.' At least that's what I anticipate.

There's a bedroom for each of us. Neither very big, but it'll be a definite plus to have a snore-proof wall between us. Extra sheets and blankets in a linen closet, sharing space with a Costco-sized bale of toilet paper. COVID panic buying has stretched deep into rural Newfoundland.

I leave Nick to make up his bed and unpack whatever clothes and gadgets he brought with him, while I finally face what was Lyle's last place of undisturbed rest.

True to Randy's word, the bed is unmade. That might have been as Lyle left it, but there's no doubt the cops thoroughly searched the room. The dresser drawers and closet are now empty, and I suspect their contents were packed away and forwarded to his parents.

I carefully strip the bed, an eye out for anything the cops might have missed. It is not a pleasant task. Young men, without parental oversight, are not known for the frequency of their sheet changing. Finding nothing but evidence of lax hygiene, I toss the offending bed linens in a corner and replace them with something considerably fresher, covering the mattress with a second fitted sheet for added peace of mind.

A few short days ago this room was the intimate territory of the murder victim. I lie tentatively across the bed, suppressing eerie in favour of bizarre. Then attempt to dwell on the unparalleled opportunity it presents to transport my mind back to where Lyle's must have been.

It's drifting in that direction when a car pulls into the driveway, sending Gaffer into full bark frenzy. As the car reverses and drives off, our housemate enters, ignoring Gaffer's warmhearted clambering at his leg, and sets a half-dozen Corona in the humming fridge. He stands back, unsmiling.

'I wasn't counting on a dog.' His hospitable nature in a tough fight to find itself.

'Gaffer is no ordinary dog.' I leave it at that.

Nick, on the other hand, squares up for the counterpunch. 'We had a go at your dishes. We're just about to make supper. Spicy ginger beef. You good with that?'

I remember the single's mindset. Arriving back at your grubby apartment, half-starved, anticipating nothing but beer and a bag of Doritos.

Randy fakes hesitation to save face. He also knows he'll never be able to suffer through the smell of cooking that is about to waft through the house.

'Sure.' My bet is he'll work himself up to a thank-you somewhere between dinner and dessert.

Food may well prove the ace up my sleeve. If Randy is going to open up to me about Lyle, then we'll need to be on better terms. It'll take time. Spicy ginger beef over a bed of linguine, garnished with lemon zest and green onion, is a good first step.

'Thank you,' he says when I put in front of him a dish of fruit salad, topped with vanilla ice cream drizzled with maple syrup. His concession in under the wire, and an opening to a slight push forward.

A benign question. 'How'd you get into acting?'

'Did theatre at Grenfell College. In Corner Brook.'

Not surprising, but not a story he's about to add to.

Instead, he turns it on me. 'How'd you know Donna?' In other words, what was my connection that got me the job.

I explain the Arts and Culture Centre bit, and add, 'Late in the season. She was desperate.'

Self-deprecation sometimes helps. Not in this case. He could do better than smug silence.

'Come Labour Day, and it will all be said and done.' If he can't tolerate us and our meals until then the fellow has a major problem. If that problem in any way played a role in Lyle's death then it needs my attention.

He checks his phone. 'My girlfriend is on the way here. I'd appreciate it if you give us some space.'

Space? Like fifty percent of the square footage. Nick catches my eye, raises his eyebrows.

'We'll remain in the vicinity of the kitchen sink,' Nick says.

I suppress an eager smirk. Randy moves to the couch. We wait out the arrival of the girlfriend, expecting the worst.

The young lady who steps past the door lights up a lacklustre room. She opens with a broad smile. And a prolonged and affectionate encounter with Gaffer. Go figure.

Gaffer returns the favour tenfold. Nick restrains him, but Jess insists he be let loose to continue his enthusiastic meet-and-greet.

I'd seen Jess playing the fiddle in the show, but, until now, we hadn't been introduced. I expected a girlfriend to complement Randy's brooding temperament. But no, Jess Simard is easygoing, personable, intent on making us part of the summer troupe.

And in the process draws out a side of Randy we haven't yet seen. A bearable side. One that volunteers information.

'We met at Grenfell,' he says.

'We ignored each other, up to this summer.' She laughs and embraces Randy at the same time. 'I thought he was a bit of an ass, to be honest.' Laughs again.

I'm liking this girl more and more.

It seems enough time has passed that Jess has been able to distance herself from what happened to Lyle. She goes there voluntarily, as if things need to be said if I'm going to feel comfortable in the acting job.

'Nobody thinks you're pushing the memory of Lyle aside. Donna had to salvage this season as best she could. Someone had to take over his part and what she tried first was hopeless.'

I appreciate that. There's more.

'I'll be honest. Some of us had issues with Lyle. We tolerated him, but he was a slacker. He didn't pull his weight. Okay, the parts he played were fine, but there weren't many of them, not compared to what most of us were dealing with. He got away with it because Donna had too many other things on her mind to see it happening.'

'Stoned half the time,' Randy throws in, 'if you want to know the truth.'

'Really?'

'He had this ability to snap out of it when he was onstage, in front of an audience.'

'And the roles he did have were lightweight, comic characters. If he messed up a line it could look like it was intentional.'

'He learned how to slip under Donna's radar. Talk his way into looking busy, while the rest of us were left with the extra parts.'

'His parents showed up with homemade jams and jellies and bottled moose, all for Donna. Talk about suckin' up.'

Might as well be blunt and see where it gets me. 'I don't get it. How could that have anything to do with him being murdered.'

'He had time on his hands,' says Jess. 'Who knows what he did with it.'

A trigger for Randy. 'That was another thing that bugged me. The shows he was in were scheduled Wednesday to Saturday. Once we were through rehearsals and everything was up and running, he had three consecutive days off, while the rest of us were lucky if we got two.'

'Any idea where he went?'

'Who knows. He had a car, and he wasn't telling me.'

Randy and Jess are gone then, off somewhere in Jess's car, doing what twenty-somethings do on a summer's evening. While I get back to Solomon Noddy.

Nick runs the lines with me before he takes to his room for the night, Gaffer in tow, my confidence as an actor having reached a new high. I spewed the lines like clockwork. All is good.

I'm due the well-deserved dram as I stand outside in the dark. It's a clear night, moonlight illuminating the slow-moving river that divides Trouty and empties into the ocean a short distance away. It's a scheduled salmon river, an exceptional feature for a Newfoundland community. And unique in the way it shelters the boats when they're not heading out to open water. Fishing sheds and wharves line the river's banks, a far cry from what I normally call home.

St. John's has its own flavour, but it's outport Newfoundland that's the mainstay of the island's character. Could I live here year-round? Probably not. But there's no denying the lure of the place on a warm summer's night. Only a deadbeat townie wouldn't admit to it.

I want this for Nick as much as for me. He's got to experience the bays and inlets of this island if he's going to call himself a Newfoundlander. Its rural life is remarkable and rare. He needs to know it and come to love it.

Now, in the midst of it all, is murder. Which only goes to show that the dark side of human nature can lurk in the most tranquil of places. Perhaps drawn here because nobody expects it.

In fact this stretch of Trinity Bay has an ample history of clandestine crime. Not far from Trouty is the island of Ireland's Eye, once a thriving fishing community, abandoned in the era of resettlement in the 1960s. Twenty years later—$225 million of Lebanese hash and the largest drug bust ever in Eastern Canada! An operation masterminded by the Montreal Mafia. Hundreds of bundles of the stuff landed by boat, then stored in decaying buildings before being ferried to trucks waiting on the mainland. Hidden under a stockpile of onions and routed to Montreal, before ending up on the streets of New York.

The talk at the time was that some bundles went unaccounted for, that local laddios hired to transport it stashed some away for themselves. To sell when the Mafia was long gone and Ireland's Eye went back to being abandoned. An outport might look idyllic, but scratch its surface with easy money, and there lurk greed, envy, wrath, any combination of the seven deadlies. Shooting your image of the peaceable, law-abiding Newfoundlander all to hell.

Which works me up enough that I phone Ailsa.

'Bit late, I know.'

'Where are you?' Sounding like she wasn't exactly standing by, waiting for my call.

I keep it upbeat. Chipper, full of confidence that I know what I've gotten myself into.

'Acting? Like on stage acting?'

Is that such a stretch? 'You'd like my Solomon Noddy.'

She's momentarily at a loss for words. 'Above and beyond the call of duty.' The closest she comes to endorsing my investigative tactics.

In need of a wakeup call in that case. 'I'm staying in the same house that Lyle Mercer had occupied. My fellow actors are proving a very valuable resource.'

I detect interest, but still not enough to confirm there's merit to what I'm about.

A non-committal 'In what way exactly?'

'In several ways.' Coyness. I like the control. There's a trace of a smile that she is not party to.

'You're not being helpful.'

'Ailsa, at this point in the game it would be premature to say where it is leading me. I want to be certain that what I turn over to you is concrete evidence. But rest assured that could come any day.'

I'm waiting for her to say I'm full of bullshit, because there's a good chance that's what she's thinking.

An exit is in order. 'Just wanted to touch base. Anything I should know from your end before I go?'

'I can't say there is.'

'No problem. Don't hesitate to call.'

A failed attempt to ease out with a little dry humour. 'Good night, then.'

By this time I've become excellent at enduring the wait for the response she is considering.

'Good night.'

That wasn't all bad. The channel remains open. Which was the whole point.

So it goes. And now for a first night in the bed formerly occupied by the murder victim.

There are times as a PI when you put yourself out there, you plunge beyond your comfort zone in the knowledge that risk has the potential to break a case wide open. No guts, no glory.

No sweat, no applause. My Solomon Noddy proves a winner. Doesn't exactly bring the house down, but hey, when I exit the stage with the rest of the gang after the piece is concluded, the hand-clapping is nothing if not robust. While not for me alone, it's music to our collective ears.

'You were fine,' says Randy, in the midst of his hurried wardrobe change for his next bit in the program. Since it's coming from Randy, I can quite easily elevate the compliment a few notches.

I don't have a next bit, other than as a stand-in among a group of backup singers. To help fill the stage. Donna has discreetly told me to mouth the words, given that my abilities as a singer are yet to be verified.

Enough to say I think I do very well as voiceless background. What I lack in vocalization I more than make up for in facial and hand gestures.

My acting chops resurface in the *Pageant*. Yes, now that Donna is satisfied with my debut in *Shenanigans*, she sees no reason for me not to take over Lyle's roles in the theatrical parade about town. Bit parts to some, but energy for the minor roles equal to that for major ones is the trait of a true professional.

The great outdoors proves a terrific benefit. A missed cue, a misplaced line—all lost to the wind and the general flurry of actors set against the Newfoundland landscape. There's no time to linger between segments. Put one role behind me, and then on to the next. By the time the show reaches its end, I've morphed into a half-dozen different characters.

And, let it be said, come through with flying colours. Standing atop the hill, decked out in a jerkin and pantaloons, vigorously waving some colonial flag as the audience breaks into its final chorus of applause—it's a fitting end to a memorable first foray into the *Pageant*.

Nick and Gaffer have traipsed about with the crowd, taking in the whole two hours. From time to time I caught a glimpse of the young man and his dog huddled together, relishing the comic moments in particular, Gaffer occasionally emitting a generous yelp. One of the more vocal fans.

'You stumbled through a few lines,' says Nick in the car, on our way back to Trouty, 'but not bad.'

Always pragmatic, that boy. 'I love you, too.'

'And guess what else?'

'I know. I messed up on one of the costume changes. The head scarf didn't really fit the church scene.'

'Donna offered me a part in the *Pageant*,' he says in a flurry. 'I gotta go to the costume department to get fitted. And Gaffer too, only I gotta come up with an old piece of rope for a lead.'

'Really?' That's good of her. I think.

'Not a speaking part. Just walk about with the other actors. You know, act like I'm from back in the day. Add to the atmosphere, as Donna put it.'

She's taken a shine to him, and the kid's pumped. 'Go for it, I'd say.'

'I promise not to upstage you.'

He's covered all the angles. I can only chuckle. 'Thanks, pal.'

'These opportunities don't come along every day.'

What is it with kids these days? He's already picturing himself walking the red carpet?

'Looks good on a résumé,' he says.

'Start building it early, why don't you.'

'I figure I should. Wouldn't hurt.'

Good God, he doesn't get that it was meant to be a joke. When I was that age I would never have heard the word "résumé", let alone been able to pronounce it.

Tempting though it is to inject a few well-chosen words about jumping into acting solely for the fun of it, I bite my tongue. Add it to my ever-growing list of gripes about the teenage mind, and set it aside. Haven't got the energy. Not worth the hassle.

What energy I do have is taken up with Ig, neighbour-of-choice. We're just in the driveway and the man is halfway across the road.

We're out of the car and he's within the standard two metres. 'Sebastian, I'd like a few words with you.'

I catch Nick's eye. He shrugs, then leads an equally reluctant Gaffer into the house.

'Guess what.'

What exactly? Ig's eagerness is unmistakable, yet I hardly expect anything earth-shattering.

'The cops were by again. With a warrant to do a second search of the property.'

'Really?' What is this? Ailsa put a crack team of rural cops back on the road? How come?

'They did a lot of swabbing.'

Ig pauses for effect.

'In what is now your bedroom, I assume.'

'Looking for?' Looking for evidence they missed the first time, some bit that I might have uncovered?

'Residue is my guess.'

Residue. Of what? They must realize the bedroom has been compromised by my moving in there.'

Suddenly I'm hit by the thought of what personal residue I might have left behind. Besides a few drops of Scotch that I spilled when I last poured the Laphroaig? It would, at least, enliven the mundane life of some lab technician.

'Actually they were just as interested in searching outside the house.'

Again he pauses, seeming to relish the further stir of my interest level.

'Looking for a spot that had recently been dug up. That's what I figure.'

'Really, Ig?'

He jumps in with both feet. 'Drugs, what else. Ecstasy,

coke, angel dust—you name it.'

Ig has been watching way too much television.

'Did they find anything?'

'Not for me to know. I scouted around after they left. Nothing disturbed that I could see. Which doesn't mean anything. I expect them to show up any minute with a sniffer dog.'

'They told you that?'

'It only stands to reason, Sebastian.'

I would say his reasoning powers have seen better days. 'If I were you, Ig, I wouldn't hold my breath.'

My next breath has been released all of five seconds when a hefty RCMP Ford SUV turns a corner and comes within sight of us standing in the driveway. It pulls off the road and parks. Two officers step out of the vehicle.

'Sergeant Simmons,' Ig intones. 'You're back.'

'Yes, Mr. Payne. And this is Corporal Watten, who has brought along . . .'

'A sniffer dog.'

There's a short but unmistakable yelp from inside the SUV.

Ig can barely contain himself. He owns the house after all. He looks convinced it has been a den for a drug dealer.

'What's his name?'

'*Her* name, Mr. Payne, is Siren.'

'I see,' says Ig. 'I thought all sniffer dogs were male.'

'That used to be the case,' Corporal Watten informs him. 'Males are naturally more independent. They don't mind being away from their handlers.'

'Just ask the missus,' Ig quips, chuckling. But failing to get an equivalent response.

It has slipped past the corporal, overly preoccupied with demonstrating his knowledge of dog handling to the general public, something which he likely doesn't get as much opportunity to do as he would like. 'Female dogs now make up roughly

15% of our service units across the country. And that's on the rise. As it turns out females make better searchers. They're more thorough. You might say they have a dogged determination to find the evidence.'

His own quip, in turn, slips past Ig. 'Not surprised,' Ig says, his mind likely still on his missus.

Siren makes her appearance, a black-and-tan German shepherd. Not unexpectedly, a good-looking dog, meticulously groomed, her coat showing a striking sheen.

She hardly has her four paws to the ground when there erupts a torrent of barking from behind the front door of the house. Gaffer has sensed an intruder on what he has come to think of, in the brief period he has resided here, as his territory. He's jumping mad, his head appearing and disappearing in the windowed upper third of the door.

I had no idea he could jump that high. More credit to him. His declaration is clear: beware the fellow canine with the audacity to challenge him.

There is only one solution—retire Gaffer to another part of Trouty while Siren goes about her business. After the officers lead Siren to the back of the house, I load the squirming, exasperated barker in my arms and make my way down the road and out of sight.

Only to return momentarily, leaving Nick to walk the indignant Gaffer. I can't be missing out on what his nemesis might discover.

Which turns out to be nothing, inside or outside the house, other than a dirty T-shirt that I suddenly remember using to clean up the Scotch spilled on the dresser. I had discovered the T-shirt under the bed. Belonged to Lyle I assumed, and overlooked by the cops during their first go-round. I had used it, then kicked it back under the bed and out of sight.

My first thought is the dog has an excellent nose for Scotch.

My second thought is his trainer is checking on the very off-chance it has traces of myclobutanil.

I reach this conclusion at a distance. It goes without saying the RCMP wants to take care of business without Joe Public hovering over them. Except, of course, I'm more than your ordinary citizen.

'Find anything, Sergeant Simmons, other than the T-shirt?' I ask casually once the canine's sniff through the property has ended.

'Yet to be confirmed, Mr. . . .' He glances at his notes. 'Synard.'

He's mispronounced it, as if it were French. I correct him and move on. 'I'll be sure to tell Inspector Bowmore that you and Corporal Watten, and Siren of course, have done an excellent job.'

He looks at me with something less than gratitude in his eyes.

Ig joins us at that moment, practically out of breath in his rush back across the road once he realized Siren's work was complete.

'Thanks, Mr. Payne, for your cooperation. We appreciate being able to go about our business uninterrupted.'

As opposed to me standing next to my car with arms folded and thinking I'm entitled to an explanation of what transpired considering it is my own personal space and that of my son that was being subjected to Siren's hair-trigger nose.

'My wife asked me to pass along her regards,' Ig says, 'and she'd like you to have a few of her tea buns. Fresh out of the oven.' Ig extends a hand bearing a small gift bag. The aroma overwhelms the moment.

Outport suck-up at its most blatant.

'We really shouldn't, Mr. Payne. It is RCMP policy . . .'

'I have to say," Ig interjects, 'if there's one thing Trouty learned from Hurricane Igor, it's the value of a good tea bun. Some women are still getting requests from members of the Canadian Military who repaired our bridge.'

The aroma does in the weak-willed. The sergeant shamelessly draws the bag from Ig's hand and lets it hang from his side in unforgivable proximity to his holstered handgun.

The men and dog are back aboard their SUV, and after some tight manoeuvring, manage to turn around and point themselves out of town. I would say the tea buns won't make it past Trinity. Scoffed down, the evidence of the gift bag conveniently disposed of.

'What's your take?' Ig says to me as I text Nick to tell him the coast is clear.

'What do you mean?'

'Doesn't it seem odd to you they didn't ask you more questions when they showed up? Like they knew you already. I didn't tell them much, other than that someone had moved in. Didn't even tell them your names.'

Ig's senses, aging though they might be, are on high alert.

'Are you an undercover cop by chance?'

Yes, and sharper than I gave him credit for.

I'd rather not be telling him I'm anything other than an actor. Thankfully, Nick and Gaffer are back. I pivot to them and escape the question.

'Did they find anything?' Nick says.

'Not for me to know.' I'm sounding appropriately naïve.

'She'll be in touch,' Nick says.

Music to Ig's ears.

Nick suddenly clicks into the fact he's poked a hole in my cover. He smiles stiffly and redirects himself and Gaffer into the house.

Ig is not smiling. 'She?'

My relationship with Ig has landed at a critical juncture.

Either I attempt to lie my way out of this, or I usher him into my confidence and trust he's got the smarts to keep it to himself.

His intensity hasn't abated. The latter choice wins out.

Ig is excited. It's as if I've redefined his role in life. As if I've deputized him, made him my second-in-command.

He holds up a fist. 'My lips are sealed,' rather too serious, but there it is. 'Nobody. Not even the missus. Especially not the missus.'

Hard fist bump. Embarrassing, only on my part.

Ig continues to defy expectations. Yes, way too much screen time.

He can't wait. Deputized and, apparently, primed for action.

'You and Nick want a go at catching a few cod the next time I go out?' He seems to have a need to pay me back.

Actually, I'm not about to turn that down. I'd love a trip out in a boat, get some of that salt air in my lungs. And Nick, I know, would be all over it. 'Absolutely.'

Another, equally hard fist bump and Ig is off, across the road. Appetite primed for a fresh tea bun.

There's a lot to be said for patience. For reflection. For the PI sitting on the couch after son and dog have gone to bed, taking time to weigh what he knows against what he doesn't. Revitalizing plans in his search for leads.

Or letting them come to him. In the form of Randy, who has shown up disgruntled (for what reason, I don't ask, if in fact he needs one) but willing, after some hesitation, to join me for a measure of the smoky dram.

Scotch has yet to enter his life in any meaningful way. I'm not surprised, given his age and attention span. Generally, single malts are wasted on the young. They wouldn't take the time to sip, pause, and reflect on what has passed over their taste buds. They are too busy getting laid and wasted.

Lucky is the young man befriended by a Scotch fiend willing to share his bottle and know-how. Lucky is the young man experiencing his first pour of Lagavulin 16. I envy the virginal single-malt drinker. Never again is a swallow quite so transformational.

It catches in his throat. He coughs slightly.

Concealed amusement on my part. I call it the cough of the innocent.

'Relax. Take your time. Hold up the glass, admire the colour, then swirl it a little, take note of how it clings to the glass. Nose it gently, become versed in the aromas. Then a moderate sip. Let it linger on your tongue, then in the back of your mouth. Savour the complexity of its flavours. Swallow only when the urge has elevated. Immerse yourself in the slow descent. Breathe. Relax.'

'You're serious? Reminds me of yoga.' Thoughtful pause. 'Kinda like sex, in a way?'

I let that pass.

'No seriously, that's a big investment for a bit of liquor.'

So very innocent. 'I assure you it's worth it.'

By the third sip he starts to come around. 'I'm liking the smoke.'

I explain the process of burning peat in the malting process, on the path to distillation. It sparks more interest.

'Do they come any smokier?'

'Way more.'

'Wicked. Not quite like smoking weed, but getting there.'

His point of reference leaves me struggling for comment.

'Lyle would have loved it,' he says.

'Enjoyed his toke, like you said.' I smile, encouragement for more.

Randy takes another sip, stretching out the time to swallowing. 'Although . . .'

'Although . . .'

'Breathe. Relax.'

No need to gloat, Randy.

'Although it was more than a toke,' he says finally. 'Lyle called it "a boost to meditation". He had his favourite spot for it.'

Randy takes another extended sip of the Scotch. To borrow a term often used by my impatient father, the wait calls for "the patience of Job".

It's worth it. 'An hour before a show, like clockwork, he'd wander off along the footpath behind the theatre. It's part of a walking trail. I followed him once out of curiosity. He sank into a spot that looked out over the bay. Below what they call Lower Gun Hill, out of sight of anyone who passed by. Anyway, I caught up with him, figured we could share a toke. "I need time alone," he says to me. "I'll see you later." That was Lyle. Made no bones about it—he had his time to meditate and that was where it worked for him, by himself.'

'How did you figure it was meditation?'

'A few days later we were smoking up, right here, where we're sitting now. Shooting the shit about what pot we'd tried and he told me he had this one strain he used exclusively before he meditated on that spot off the trail.'

'Sounds like Lyle had a lot going on in his head he was trying to get rid of.'

'I did wonder if sitting there, looking out the bay, if suicide ever entered his mind. Like dive into the bay and drown himself.'

'It happens.' Intentional drowning is not uncommon. Tough way to go, though, when you think of it.

Randy draws back. 'I kinda doubt it now. Just that to me it looked like his head was filled with shit that had nothing to do with acting. Like he worked himself into a job with Rising Tide for some other reason.'

Never considered that. 'Interesting premise.'

Randy finishes what remains in his glass. He sets it on an end table and stares at me. 'Premise?'

Maybe not the best word choice. Sounding a bit investigative. 'You know, like . . .'

'Like you're another one who worked yourself into a job with Rising Tide for some other reason?'

So. Ah. There's the rub, as my confidant Hamlet would say. I'm not all that surprised. Randy is, I've come to realize, more perceptive than I first gave him credit for. Rather like Ig.

'And what are you suggesting that reason might be?'

'You tell me.'

Attempting to blow my cover. I could come clean, or I could try to bullshit my way past it. Given that the second option would likely only bolster his level of suspicion, I give in.

'Are you good with intrigue?'

He continues to stare at me, but now rather blankly.

'Can you keep a lid on what I'm about to tell you?'

'Go for it.'

I take that as a vote of confidence that I'm doing the right thing.

'I'm a private investigator looking into Lyle's murder.'

He chews on that for a while. 'Which makes me a suspect.'

I don't deny it. 'Everyone's a suspect. Some more so than others. I'll say this much in your favour—I'd be uncomfortable if I thought Nick and I were sleeping in the same house as a murderer. We're still here.'

'Thanks,' he says dryly.

'No problem.'

'Who hired you? Let me guess.'

'That will remain unsaid.'

'Now I get why she gave you a job when there are so many real actors out of work.'

I secretly snarl at the dig while managing to remain tight-lipped.

We've reached a standstill. Not much to do but put the cork stopper back in the Lagavulin and call it a night.

Randy heads to his bedroom, but with one last comment. 'I wasn't crazy about Lyle, but I had absolutely no reason to kill him. It wasn't me.' His hand on the doorknob, he adds, 'But I'm game to help you find out who did, if that's what you want. Good night.'

'Good night.' But his door is closed already.

SCENE 2

THE INVESTIGATION NEEDS an injection of adrenalin from the top—a sit-down, focused one-on-one with Donna.

Before I know it the summer season will be over, the whole company disbanded, scattered to the four winds, ready access to key players in the case suddenly out of reach.

Time to get my rear in gear. Seize the friggin' day.

The first step, setting up a meeting with Donna, hits a brick wall. She would have me think her plate's perpetually full. There's no denying she's constantly on the move, as we're prone to saying in Newfoundland, "like a blue-arsed fly".

'Donna, twenty minutes, that's all. We need a reality check.'

A poorly timed chuckle as she breezes past. 'Check my reality and you'll get more than you bargained for.'

Finally, two hours later, she wedges me in.

Five minutes of small talk, and suddenly she's laser-focused on what my muckraking has revealed so far. Only when I get to the bit about Lyle's pot-enhanced meditation habit is her concentration broken.

'Meditation? He was supposed to be writing a script, not wasting his time smoking dope and making peace with the bloody universe.'

'Script?'

'Didn't I tell you?'

Like I said, too much on her plate.

'Part of the deal when I hired him was to finish up a script, a new play, for next season. I cut back on his acting roles to give him extra time to write.'

So he wasn't such a slacker after all. 'Lyle was a playwright?'

'That remained to be seen. He had written about twenty pages. It wasn't bad. Set in Trinity in the 1970s—that appealed to me. I like doing plays with local connections.'

'What was it about?'

'A bunch of students in the last weeks of high school. Where it was leading I couldn't quite tell and he didn't want to say at that point. I trusted him. His characters were well drawn and it had a definite momentum. Teenagers trying to make up their minds about what they wanted to do with their lives. Dialect mixed with the lingo and music from the 70s—he had it down pat. The draw of the mainland versus staying here. The universal Newfoundland theme, but from a different angle.'

'Did he get through a first draft?'

'Who knows. We were supposed to meet to talk about it. Never happened.'

I wonder why. 'The cops must have his laptop. Likely it's on that. It might offer some clues about the murder. I need to have a look.'

'You want me to ask?'

'Better coming from you than me.' I rifle through my notebook and produce the phone number of the RCMP detachment in Bonavista. She resists the pressure to act quickly. I persist. 'We've no time to play with.'

Donna takes off her glasses and brings her cell closer to her face, punching in the numbers. Her call is directed to the sergeant in short order.

'How are you?' Pause. 'You know, trying to stay sane. It's a challenge.' Fractured laughter. 'I see schools are opening up for September. Hilda will be relieved.'

It becomes clear that Donna and Sergeant Simmons (and Hilda, who I surmise is the good sergeant's spouse) have known each other for years, their acquaintance only reinforced by recent events. I shouldn't be surprised. Donna has a wide network.

It could well prove profitable when, five minutes later, she finally gets to the matter of the laptop. Donna leads with one sharp line of persuasion. Rising Tide is struggling through a tough season, it needs a strong comeback next year if the company is going to survive, and that means fresh new material to draw bigger audiences. Including the play she had commissioned from Lyle Mercer which she assumes is on his laptop. Is it? And how soon can the RCMP get a copy of it to her?

She cleverly traded "if" for "when". The anticipation of the response from Sergeant Simmons hangs in the air. Not for long.

'Really?' she says. 'That was it.'

Donna tosses me a pen and makes a writing motion. I jot down the phone number she repeats.

'And who should I ask for?' she says.

No need. I recognize the number. I fill in the name before she dispenses it, and when she does, I offer up a smile, broad but artificial. She looks at me and raises her eyebrows.

Donna gives the sergeant a subdued good-bye and drops the cell to her desk.

She seems perplexed. 'No laptop,' she says. 'Mini iPad, iPhone, but no laptop.'

'Really. That can't be right. They all have laptops.'

I grab my phone and drop Randy a quick text. He's back to me within seconds.

'Randy says he did have one.'

'Whatever the cops confiscated is in St. John's for analysis. Simmons says maybe it's on the iPad. Ask your friend . . . Ailsa.'

Which frees Donna to get back to running the theatre company. 'You know the pitch,' she says to me as I exit her office. Then adds, 'Use your charm.'

As close as it gets to a vote of confidence. Not that I need one. My acquaintance with Ailsa should be enough to secure a copy of the script, if in fact there is one, somewhere.

I'm sitting on the wharf bench outside the theatre, ready to dial. Nobody around. Calm. No wind. Still waters, running deep.

'How are you?' A neutral opening line. Playing it safe until I gauge the lie of the land, in view of the fact our relationship is still grappling with its challenges.

'Good,' she says. 'Yourself?'

'You know. Slow but steady.'

'Something's up?' Needlessly curt.

'As a matter of fact . . .' Pause. I'm determined to slow the pace, build her anticipation. 'I've discovered Lyle was into meditation.'

'Really.' Deadpan. 'That's it?'

I push forward. 'It would appear he had a lot going on in his head other than acting.'

'Really. What exactly?'

'In that regard, was there a laptop among his personal items?'

Eventually, 'Not that I'm aware of.'

Meaning no. 'But there was an iPad. It could turn out to be hugely significant.'

And with that the pitch begins, the aforementioned charm in motion. Ailsa might display the no-nonsense front on which the RCMP built its reputation, but beneath it is an inspector who knows full well that the case comes first, and she is not about to take a chance on what leads might emerge from a PI in the thick of it, playing the ground game.

'We were wondering why he had written it and if it's of any use.'

So there is something on the iPad after all. I'm surprised. But, yes, lucky break. And the script is also on their radar. 'Once I see it I'll fill you in.'

'With what, exactly?'

'That depends. I'll need to see it first.'

She weighs what she might gain by sending it to me, versus what she might lose.

It's obvious there's nothing to lose. But it goes against police psyche to give in that easily. It plays havoc with their self-image. Like it would be earth-shattering to relinquish a sliver of control.

Might as well put it all on the table. 'You're worried I might find something and go marching off to investigate without telling you. And screw up evidence in the process.'

I'm waiting for it.

'Exactly.'

'Exactly what do you take me for, Ailsa? You think I'm an idiot playing some half-assed game for fun, without a clue what I'm doing? Is that it? You think I don't know evidence when I see it and haven't got the sense to turn it over to the cops when I know it would help solve the case?'

She doesn't answer right away and I'm not about to give her time to think about it any longer. 'I have to go. Call me if you ever get it in your mind you want to talk.' A short breath. 'Good-bye.'

I cut the line and fume.

Fuck, either she trusts me or she doesn't. The shit bloody well needed to hit the fan.

So I likely did the job on myself. So fucking what. There it is. Done.

I fume even more. The still waters, no matter how bloody deep, are no bloody help.

The phone dings. Text message.

From Ailsa. *Okay. Expect it later today.*

Sometimes impulsiveness pays. Enough said.

Nick takes my attention. The kid has spent the last hour getting rigged out for his part in the *Pageant*. He's been higher than a kite since he crawled out of bed this morning. When I show up to see how his fitting has gone, I find the three women who run the costume department, two of an age to be his grandmother and all happily fussing over him, making last-minute adjustments so what will emerge on the byways of Trinity this afternoon is a kid who looks to be straight off a nineteenth-century fishing stage. Nick, for his part, has charmed them for all he's worth.

'By rights I should go barefoot,' he says, 'but look at these,' raising a foot to show me the scrap leather moccasins moulded to fit over and disguise his checkerboard Vans. 'Cool or what?'

Gaffer is not impressed. The dog has claimed space under a worktable to hide after his coat was muddied with makeup, to match the dirty piece of frayed rope tied around his neck. Gaffer's pride has been compromised, but he'll no doubt rise to the occasion once thrust into the limelight.

Donna has been coaching them both. Her ability to bring out the best in the actors she hires is legendary, but I doubt if she's ever worked with the four-legged variety. Given that Gaffer is prone to barking at inappropriate times, Nick has assured her that he'll have him well in hand. As for Nick himself, the lad appears to have soaked in every last word of Donna's directions. After all, a career in theatre is at stake. (No,

I shouldn't laugh. One of the actors from a few seasons past has, sure enough, ended up on Broadway.)

When their *Pageant* debut arrives, boy and dog together blossom into a star side attraction. Their role is to move about with the audience, at a suitable social distance, and without being a distraction from the scenes themselves. Nick has morphed into a grimy urchin with an odd version of a cockney accent (picked up, no doubt, from our many hours of watching Monty Python). Gaffer, dog that he is, demonstrates no need to keep his distance. He stretches the full length of his rope and rollicks in the attention coming from the legion of dog lovers in the audience. He's a ham and a half.

At the end of the *Pageant*, the pair takes a spot among the actors for the final bow. The smile across Nick's face is unending. I haven't seen him flying this high in a long time. Broadway beckons.

When we get back to Trouty I make straight for my computer. The script is there all right. Inspector Bowmore has made good on her promise.

The first line of the accompanying email is business as usual. *Let me know if anything triggers a lead.* The second (and last) line not so much. *I'll be in Trinity next week.*

The investigation requires the top gun to move in. Good. Our differences of opinion will no longer require a long-distance phone call. They could do with getting up front and personal. Time will tell.

We've picked up supper on the way back. What I call the McCain desperate quick fix. Pizza pockets and five-minute fries. We both balk, but the taste buds will have to be put on standby until morning.

While we pick and swallow I text Randy for permission to use his printer. He gets back with a generous "k".

Nick sets it up so my laptop will speak to Randy's printer and eventually the latter starts the spew of pages. I'm all-fire eager to settle in for an evening of in-depth analysis.

The spew stops prematurely. I check the paper tray, then check the computer file. Jolt. It runs to twenty pages.

That's it. I retrieve the pages and take a look at the top one. It reads "preliminary draft". It's dated four months earlier. It dawns on me that what I have in my hands is the same twenty pages that Lyle showed Donna. Nothing more. That anything he added to it must be on his laptop.

Wherever the fuck that ended up. I'm burning to talk to Randy.

In the meantime I pore over the pages, pen in hand, looking for something, anything that might trigger more questions.

I take the few pages to be a set-up, for what's about to unfold at the core of the play. It starts at a high school grad dance with banter typical of the 1970s, overlaid with a bad cover version of *Stairway To Heaven*. (Cringe. All uphill from here, I'm thinking.)

An exchange of insults between a couple of loudmouths and their nerdy prey is adeptly calmed by the DJ spinning another 70s jewel, *You're The One That I Want*. (Cringe. Although, to be fair, the decade didn't give Lyle much to work with.)

It draws the now horny loudmouths to the dance floor with what I suspect is a pair of Olivia Newton-John look-alikes. (I will admit I always had a bit of a thing for Olivia, who was getting *Physical* by the 1980s, just when I lurched into puberty. That song was enough to give a teenage boy the sweats, if I recall correctly.)

The dance fades to an end with *Feel Like Makin' Love* by Bad Company. (Foreshadowing if I ever saw it.) The loudmouths are finally silenced. Lost in their lust, having fastened themselves firmly to their girlfriends, open palms gripping rounded butts.

Thankfully, we move to Scene Two.

Set change. Open space. Beach in Trinity. Secluded. (My eager pen quickly underlines the last few words. Why Trinity specifically?)

Fake fire. Ocean waves in the near distance. Post-grad beach party. Beer and pot lubricating the banter. This time it runs to who's off to trade school, who to university. Who can't leave Newfoundland fast enough, straight to Alberta. What few are staying put, for now. The age-old story Donna had talked about. Economic reality robbing the outports of their youth.

Lyle's script, however, seems to be moving beyond that, to something more, though at this point there's no telling quite what. The characters are deepening, their prejudices intensifying. One of them, who looked pretty wimpish to me in the opening scene, is shaping up as the intellectual, verbally outplaying the pair of assholes taunting him at every turn. By the end of the scene, he's the only one left, sitting next to the fire, drinking beer, excited at the prospect of university, pondering what the future holds. Well on by now, staggering a bit towards the water, ripping air guitar, singing a fractured version of *Raise A Little Hell*. (Cringing once more, but hanging in there.)

And, just when I'm wound up, anxious for more, the script ends. Twenty pages. *Finito*.

It's midnight before Randy comes through the door, the smell of fried chicken and beer only partially masked by the residue of his cologne.

Lyle's laptop is missing, I tell him. What else does he know? I oil his brain with a little Scotch.

'MacBook Pro.' He looks at me, expecting a reaction.

He's right, I'm impressed. I would say the model is not typical of a part-time actor/playwright with an uncertain cash flow. 'You're sure it wasn't just borrowed?'

'Who lets anyone borrow their MacBook Pro for three months? Sure as hell not anyone I know.'

'When did you see it last?'

He takes an extended sip. It works well. 'Whenever he got up in the morning he'd have a shower, then sit at the table, towel around him, eating a bowl of instant oatmeal crowned with chia seeds, hemp husks, and a blob of plain yoghurt. Never failed. That was Lyle—letting himself air dry over the same ritual breakfast, his laptop open in front of him.'

Randy paints a good picture. 'So he had it that last morning?'

'Absolutely.'

'And do you know if he took it with him when he went into Trinity that afternoon?'

'If he did he would have kept it in his backpack. It wasn't in there at the end of the show, I know that for a fact. I discovered the backpack under a pile of his regular clothes in his locker backstage, what he was wearing before he did his costume changes. When the show was over and he'd been taken to the hospital I grabbed what was in his locker and brought it back to the house. I remember the backpack felt almost empty. No laptop that's for sure.'

'Where's the backpack now?'

'The cops have it I guess. They took a bunch of his stuff from the house for analysis.'

'So the laptop could have been stolen from the backpack while he was onstage?' I'm thinking aloud.

'I assumed he hadn't taken it into Trinity, that he left it in his bedroom and eventually the cops confiscated it. So . . . maybe it was stolen.'

'More than maybe I'd say. Suppose the thief snuck into the back of the theatre from outdoors, came through the green room to the lockers . . .'

'And searched around until he found the backpack with the laptop inside?' says Randy. 'Without being seen by someone? I doubt it very much. In fact I'd say the chances are zilch.'

Suddenly we're both thinking the same thing—the theft was an inside job.

'I rise back up the list of suspects,' says Randy.

It's in my head, I'll admit.

My gut says otherwise. 'I figure at this point you're close to the bottom.' Followed by a well-intentioned shrug.

He's amused, which I take as a positive. Randy has turned the corner for me. He's no longer such a pain in the ass. We've reached an understanding, of sorts. We've reached the point of hovering, about to land on common ground.

'Who then?'

'It's plausible the laptop was stolen by someone who had nothing to do with the murder. Say someone saw Lyle with it before the show, decides to cash in on the fact the backpack must be lying around somewhere, its owner out of the picture. Maybe had an eye on it for a while. Suddenly here is a prime opportunity. Slip it out of Lyle's backpack and into his own.'

'Doubt that,' Randy says. 'Too much of a risk. Imagine if Donna found out. The fellow'd be shittin' bricks from dawn to daylight.'

Not to mention what it would do to his theatre career.

I take a few steps toward another perspective. 'Just remember, if whoever took it was the murderer, then stealing it was definitely a chance worth taking, given there might be something on the laptop that implicated him. Or her.'

Randy suppresses the urge to counterpunch and lapses into silence.

In any case the laptop is gone. And, at this point, unlikely to be recovered. Could be lying at the bottom of Trinity Bay for all we know.

What I have to work with is a twenty-page chunk of script. Randy, I discover, had no idea Lyle was writing a play.

'I guess I shouldn't be surprised,' he says. 'He spent a lot of time in the bedroom with the door closed. Good to know it was the computer he was playing with.'

I'll let that one pass. I hold up the script and give him the lowdown on what it's about. 'Anything strike you?'

'Good choice of songs.'

It might take a few years, but I'm sure his taste in music will improve.

I switch his focus. 'What beach do you figure he had in mind?'

'Secluded,' he says. 'Not much to choose from that's easily accessible. There's one he could see from where he'd sit to meditate.'

Could be making sense. 'Meditation, motivation, take time to conjure up the scenes in his head before putting pen to paper.'

'Sounds logical to me.' He shrugs.

'But I'm thinking—why Trinity? Why that particular spot? Lyle wasn't from here. Why not set it where he grew up?'

'A no-brainer. He was sucking up to Donna.'

He's probably right. 'She did say she liked the local connection.'

'But I'm willing to bet the idea for the play came from his own experience,' Randy says. 'He looked to me like the type who didn't fit in when he was in high school. Probably had the shit kicked out of him a few times. The story on stage was his way of getting back at the bastards.'

'So why set it back forty, fifty years?'

'Could be because he liked the music.'

Randy's learning curve is steeper than I thought. It's hard not to be smug.

'No, I'm serious. I used to hear Trooper through his head-phones.' Randy starts to bob to an imagined rhythm. He starts to sing *3 Dressed Up As A 9*.

Another classic piece of Canadian songwriting. Let's move on, shall we. 'Very good.' A smirk is not to be contained.

'He had them on cassettes. He showed them to me, four cassette tapes, like they were gold. And a Walkman to play them on. Ever see a Walkman? I was blown away.'

Yes, Randy, I have seen a Walkman. Yes, I owned a Walkman.

'Prized relics,' he says.

Thank you, Randy. Just remember that one day that iPhone 12 you're hoping your overly indulgent parents might give you for Christmas will be a "prized relic".

'I just don't get it,' I say. Don't get Randy's persistence. Or the cult of Trooper for that matter.

'The tapes belonged to a cousin of his who died when he was a teenager. When Lyle was about the same age, he was visiting this cousin's parents and they asked Lyle if he'd like to have the guy's music collection and device.'

'It wasn't called a "device", Randy.'

'Whatever. They'd been keeping it all those years. Apparently, Lyle looked a lot like the cousin.'

'What happened?'

'Don't know.' Randy shrugs. 'Bit weird really, when you think about it. The guy died long before Lyle was born and here was Lyle freaking out listening to the same music playing on the very same . . . piece of gear.'

'Piece of gear.' I chuckle. Not quite, Randy. "Piece of gear" had, shall we say, a very different meaning when I was his age. I chuckle again.

Randy is ready for bed. He's hung in longer than I expected. He saunters off towards his room, a raised fist sleepily pumping the air. '*We're Here For A Good Time (Not A Long Time)*. They're still on the go. I saw them a couple of years ago at the George Street Festival. Wicked.'

You know how a song worms itself into your head, no matter how much you fight it, no matter how long ago you dismissed it as mindless drivel from your fickle youth.

'Dad, what are you muttering?'

We're dog-walking along this stretch of beach where Randy figured Lyle set the scene in the play. I don't know its name, or if it even has one. I'm here to see if it triggers something, a jolt of some kind. A spark, a flash of insight which the investigation desperately needs.

And, in the meantime, Trooper is driving me crazy.

Nick releases Gaffer from his lead and the two of them chase each other down the beach. I sit on the rocks and ponder.

There's an art to pondering. It requires being able to shut out alien distractions (i.e., boy and dog) and let thoughts flow freely.

For Lyle this place conjured up a young man on the edge. Edge of what exactly? He had outplayed the bastards and now he is in for a good time?

Will he find that good time? Or will he get fucked? *Not A Long Time.*

Is he about to stumble into that water and not come out of it alive?

I need answers.

'Dad, what's up? You're lookin' a little . . . pissed.'

The aliens have returned, out of breath. 'The case, you know. Like I'm feeling well . . . like it's going nowhere.'

'Man, that's not like you.' He takes to the rocks next to me while Gaffer wanders about on a sniff session. 'Okay,' he says. 'Hit me, man. What's goin' through your head?'

Top marks for enthusiasm. What can I do but smile.

On the walk here I told him that Lyle *maybe* had a connection with the beach.

'So what else did Randy tell you?'

'Not much.' I throw in the bit about the cousin.

'Very cool. The Walkman I mean. Classic. Right up there with bell bottoms. I read about them, too.'

Sorry I opened my mouth.

'Listen, Dad, you need to do something. You can't sit around thinking all the time. It's not good for you. You gotta get up and get at it. If I were you, I'd start by finding out more about the dead cousin.'

'Who died like forty years ago.'

'Sooo.'

Logic is not a teenage strong point. We both go to mute. Generational standoff.

The dead cousin angle has all the potential of a wild goose chase. Not that I have a better suggestion.

In my own good time, an uneager 'Okay.'

His thumb fires straight up. 'I'll drink to that!'

'Not beer you won't. Kool-Aid, maybe.'

He chuckles. Then gives me the wink and nod.

SCENE 3

SOOO, NOW, WE'RE on our way to Keels. Always wanted to go to Keels. Love the name. It's on the other side of the Bonavista Peninsula, about an hour north from Trouty, as the crow drives.

Keels, as in the backbones of boats, running stem to stern. I've read that Giovanni Caboto left the imprint of his ship's keel in the sand when he stopped for a drink of fresh water in 1497. (Wishful thinking on the part of the local tourist association is my guess.)

Regardless, Keels is one of the oldest settlements in Newfoundland, going back to the 1600s. At one time over five hundred "livyers" called it home, cod-fishing families all of them. Livyer is one of my favourite Newfoundland words. Succinct, to the point, and considerably more zip than "permanent resident".

Like most Newfoundland outports, Keels no longer crowds the landscape. Population today—roughly fifty livyers.

I'm in search of two of them. Stan and Vickie Mercer, Lyle's parents. They have no idea I'm about to show up on their doorstep. I haven't called ahead. I figured that explaining over the phone who I am exactly and what I'm up to might put them off. Hard to turn me away when we stand face to face. And they're Newfoundlanders after all, teapot likely at the ready. I just hope they're home.

I need directions to the house. The Hubert & James Mesh general store is undoubtedly the best bet.

'We're from St. John's.' A calculated opening line. To let the gentleman behind the cash know it's not potentially COVID-ridden mainlanders entering his premises. 'Masks?'

'You're good.' Still, we keep a respectful distance. 'Here to see the Devil's Footprints?'

Which is a bit off-putting. The reference feels rather cultish, until we discover that said footprints are indentations in the rock faces nearby. Imprints, as legend would have it, left by the roaming, cloven-hoofed Satan himself.

I smile broadly. Another impressive tourist draw no doubt. It's somewhat anticlimactic to say we only want directions to the Mercer home.

The fellow responds without hesitation. 'Take the main road past Clayton's Chip Truck. Yellow two-storey on your right. Couldn't miss it if you were blind.' That's reassuring.

We can't leave without a show of gratitude.

'Friends of the family are you?' he says, handing back the change from two Polar Bars.

'You might say that.'

'There's been a steady stream since all this happened. Heart-breaking.'

'For sure. You knew Lyle then?'

Dumb question I realize, given the population of Keels.

'School bus dropped him off. Beeline for the shop. Never failed. He had a part in the movie.'

'The movie?' It looks as if I've missed the boat a second time.

'*Maudie*. One of the scenes was filmed here. They liked the look of the place. Thought it could easily pass for the 1950s.'

I can imagine. He points to the rear of the store. 'A new addition.' I notice the sign for the first time. *Maudie's Tea Room.*

The tourist industry initiative continues to amaze.

'Lyle, sir, what role did he play?'

'Not a role as such. They called it a walk-on. He didn't have lines as such.'

'I see.'

'But everyone who saw the movie could tell it was him, here in the shop, in the background. Besides, he and Ethan Hawke got to be great pals.'

'Ethan Hawke?'

'He acted in a movie . . . something about a dead poet . . . when he was Lyle's age. As it turned out, Lyle was obsessed with that movie.'

'Ethan Hawke.' Loved *Dead Poets Society.* I glance at Nick. Him, too. We're both a bit dumbstruck. We're also remembering the time I showed him a YouTube clip of Ethan Hawke playing Hamlet. I have to be honest—a bit of a dud.

'Nominated for an Oscar four times,' the gentleman tells us, 'for acting *and* writing. Can you imagine when *he* showed up in Keels? It was like a message from God to show Lyle his path in life.'

We head out the door, feeling like we just had an impromptu brush with fame.

It leaves me ruminating on the amazing yet untapped cinematic potential of Newfoundland. There've been a few films shot here, but I'm thinking there'll come a time when we'll be beating the movie crowd off with a stick. Where else could you find a readymade 1950s store where you'd hardly have to change a thing but the cans and the cash register?

As we walk past the Chip Truck (with a wave to Clayton), I've decided it's best if I approach the Mercer house on my own.

In any event Gaffer needs exercise. He and Nick veer off as I turn into the driveway, past a pickup and a Corolla. I assume the latter belonged to Lyle.

I knock gently rather than ring the doorbell, then step well back. More than enough time passes, but I refrain from knocking again. Eventually, a man appears behind the door's glass panel. He eases the door open and fills the gap. I guess him to be a few years older than I am. He is dressed in navy blue coveralls.

'Mr. Mercer?'

'How can I help you?'

I introduce myself. 'I'm very sorry about your son.' He doesn't respond. Coming from a stranger it doesn't mean much. 'I'm a friend of Donna. In Trinity.'

'Yes.'

'I would like to speak to you and Mrs. Mercer about Lyle, if I could. I realize it's an imposition . . .'

'What about Lyle?'

'I'm helping with the investigation. I have a few questions. It won't take long.'

His hesitation slowly eases. 'Come in.'

I take a mask out of my pocket.

He shakes his head. 'You're good.'

He steps back. I go inside and close the door behind me. He leads me to the kitchen.

Stan introduces me to Vickie, who is standing at the counter about to pour hot water into a teapot. Good timing. Though Vickie, caught unawares, quickly moves to put on a mask. Stan waves it off. 'One of the crowd from Rising Tide.'

She takes another china mug from the cupboard, and invites me to join them at the table. I sit at the opposite end. It's a fair-sized table. All is good. Stiff but good.

The informal kitchen setting does make breaking the ice

that much easier. Tea and Purity biscuits are a big help.

There are preliminaries of course—how I happened to be in the audience on the evening of Lyle's collapse, how this led to my being hired by Rising Tide (carefully avoiding the fact that I've replaced Lyle both on the stage and in the house).

'And, of course, I often work hand in hand with police departments.' Which I do. Often, if not always.

'I see,' Stan says. The first indication they might be willing to help, as hard as it is for them to speak about their son.

'Did you know Lyle was writing a play for Rising Tide?'

They appear relieved it wasn't more personal. 'About Aub, yes.'

'Aub? I'm sorry . . .'

'Aubrey, his first cousin once removed. He drowned.'

I wasn't expecting anything so quick and decisive. 'I hadn't realized . . .' The "once removed" business I can never understand.

'Aub drowned . . . must be forty years ago now. He died the night of his graduation from high school.'

To say I'm stunned would be a mild assessment.

'They were having a beach party. He was the only one left. The police report said he was drunk and somehow ended up in the water. The combination of the cold water and alcohol.'

More stunned. The free flow is far more than I anticipated. As if talking about someone's death other than Lyle's is somehow cathartic.

Vickie looks at her husband, seemingly to seek his approval. 'Our son had other ideas, Mr. Synard.'

'You have to remember . . . Lyle had a strong imagination,' Stan inserts. 'From the time he was a boy.'

Vickie forces herself to find the courage. 'Lyle thought . . . there was more to the story. He thought . . . someone made it look like Aubrey drowned. That . . . I can't say it, Mr. Synard.'

Stan rests a hand on hers, turns to me. 'Like I said—a strong imagination. He thought it could make a good play.'

Deep breath on my part. Deep breath and major turn of mind.

The missing words remain unspoken.

'Have you told the police?'

'You're the first one to ask.'

Perhaps I shouldn't be surprised. The RCMP have their expertise. Looking for clues in the dramatic arts is obviously not one of them.

'Is there anything else you can tell me about Aubrey? Where did all this happen?'

'In Trinity. I don't know exactly where.'

Deeper breath. Second major realignment. Good God.

'You mean Aubrey lived in Trinity? Not . . . some other place.'

'His family moved there the year before it happened. His father was an Anglican minister. They moved again, shortly after. You can understand why.'

Which means Lyle's meditation beach, the one Nick and I went to yesterday with Gaffer, is the very place where Aubrey drowned. Lyle wasn't just using it for inspiration. He was conjuring up what he thought happened on that beach all those years ago.

Which also means he would have asked around Trinity to find that out. 'I would say your son did a lot of research.'

'I guess,' Stan says. 'He never talked much about it, not to us. All I know is he was desperate to get a job with Rising Tide. He was determined to spend a summer in Trinity, where his cousin had lived.'

'He somehow convinced Donna to take him on,' Vickie says, 'even though he didn't have much experience acting.'

'He was doing English at MUN. He wanted to be a writer.'

'Did he say anything, anything at all, about what he found out about Aubrey?'

Vickie's voice is breaking. 'No, Mr. Synard, he didn't. That's all we know.'

I see her tears. This has been upsetting for them both, but especially Vickie. As much as I want to ask more questions, I think it best if I leave. In any case, it's doubtful there's any more to be learned by prolonging our time together.

As I push back my chair, Vickie asks me to wait for a moment. She has something to show me. She returns from another room with a framed picture.

She hands it to me without saying anything. He's wearing a graduation gown, a rolled diploma in his hand.

'Lyle Aubrey Mercer,' his father says.

I stare at the young man for a long time before setting his picture on the table.

I thank each of them. 'Let me say again how sorry I am at the loss of your son.'

'It's not sympathy we need,' Stan says abruptly, as he walks with me to the door. 'It's answers. Why would anyone do this to Lyle, you tell us that? You investigate all you want, but unless you come up with answers, then what's the use?'

It's not a reassuring walk back down the driveway. There are times, in the haste of an investigation, when you lose sight of the prime reasons you do what you do. It's not only the satisfaction of seeing the perpetrator behind bars. It's as much making it easier for the victim's family to come to terms with what has happened. It's having their questions answered. Why would anyone do this to Lyle Mercer?

Nick is on the Devil's own mission. Determined to see his Footprints. My head is nowhere near that space, but I won't try talking him out of it. It can't all be about me.

'Think of it this way,' he says as we walk past the sign point-ing us in the direction of said footprints. 'So you're a private eye, right? Tracking the Devil, right? Out sniffing around, on the hunt for the tracks he left behind.'

You raise them to be creative thinkers, you suffer bad analo-gies. It's deserving of a poke in the ribs. It doesn't deter him.

'Ah ha!' he declares as we approach a trail of circular cavities along a rock face, well above our heads. 'You come to Keels and there you have it—evidence of Satan, solid as rock!'

'Erosion.'

'Erosion? You got to be kidding. Devilry! Pure, absolute wickedness!'

He's on a roll. He's been known to do a wild impersonation of a hell-and-brimstone gospel preacher. (One guess where he picked that up.)

I'm game to play the devil's advocate. With iPhone in hand and in my best teacher voice, 'According to the Discovery Global Geopark website, and I quote, "they are cavities left where carbonate nodules, called concretions, have eroded out of the bedrock."'

'Cavities! Let the evil-doers dwell on their cavities!'

'"Concretions form early in the process that turns buried sediment into rock, as mineral cement (i.e., carbonate) is deposited in layers growing outward from a central point."'

'The central point, Mr. PI, is that where you least expect it you find evidence of the Devil. Now it's up to us to track that Devil down.'

Gotta love that kid. Gotta be forever thankful he's in my life.

Now he grips the air microphone. Launches into a Mick Jagger/*Sympathy For The Devil* routine.

It breaks me up. Like when he was a ten-year-old, hamming it up around the rec room.

Hamming it up together, like we're doing now.

'One more time.' With the Jagger head jerk.

We hadn't figured on meeting anyone. Our sheepish smiles are directed to a svelte, exercise-hungry couple just coming our way. Never knew Gore-Tex came in bright pink. They slow down momentarily, continuing to jog on the spot.

'Having a little fun,' Nick offers by way of explanation, at the same time struggling to hold a tight lead on Gaffer.

'*Sympathy For The Devil*,' I add. I try pointing to the rock face.

Neither of them thinks it's funny. Must be mainlanders. Definitely not Stones fans. New Age Nova Scotians would be my guess, let loose in the Atlantic Bubble. I have the urge to put on a mask, to see if they'll sour even more.

'We've seen it already,' announces one, as they retake the trail.

'No problemo! Enjoy your day.'

Nick and I roll our eyes in tandem. Killjoys.

One last, introspective scan of the rock face and its hoof-prints. We must press on, make our way to the car. Lucifer's tracks are left to erode some more.

Only to have the thought of them resurface as I walk past the Mercer house.

Two cousins, removed by forty years, both lives cut painfully short. Are they, in point of fact, linked? The question rattles my mind all the way back to Trinity.

And if so, just how did the devil's work span the decades?

ACT THREE

SCENE 1

WITH LABOUR DAY closing in, Rising Tide's seasonal endgame is in sight. Last traipse about town for the *Pageant*. Curtains on *Shenanigans*. Cast and crew soon scattered to the four winds.

Nick, teenage slug-a-bed, is on the go by 6 a.m. Off in the boat with Ig for another crack at the cod. It's what's called the "summer food fishery", government-regulated days in which every man and his dog are on the saltwater, hell-bent on catching their quota—five fish per person, fifteen per boat. Fresh cod for the table. Freezers full for the winter.

Nothing beats being out in an open boat in the early morning, sunlight burning off the fog. That briny scent mixed with the cries of kittiwakes and gulls. A glimpse of a porpoise, or an eagle returning to its nest. It breathes life into being a Newfoundlander.

Ig invited both of us out a few days ago. When his GPS told him we had reached his tried-and-true spot, his first priority was to instruct the young fellow on just how to go about hooking a cod. Cast out the line and let the single-hook lure drop until it strikes the bottom, reel it back up a ways, then jerk the line up and let it sink back, then again, and again until . . . sure enough, Nick hooked into one brute of a fish. There's the kid, grin the width of his face, fighting to reel in the wriggling cod, finally getting it to the surface, just as Ig scoops it into a dip net, up and over the gunnel and straight into the tub lying in the bottom of the boat.

Nick was over the moon. A half-hour later we had our quota. The kid couldn't wait to go out again.

I'm all for him doing it on his own this time, without me tagging along. I'm all for seeing him navigate his own way in the world. To give him room to grow up on his own terms.

I sit at the kitchen table with black coffee, notebook open, man on a mission. If I'm to make headway on this case between now and one final Solomon Noddy there's a hell of a lot to unravel.

My plan is to start with Donna. Aim: to trigger something about her dealings with Lyle that might just add a crucial piece to the puzzle. (And while I'm at it cool her thirst for confirmation that my slice of her budget has been money well spent.)

Nick returns, thick cod fillets tucked in the fridge. He showers and feeds, and is ready to hit the road to Trinity by 9:30. The boy naps all the way, Gaffer nestled in his arms.

No time to hang back, waiting for a time slot. I'm at the front door to the theatre when Donna's 4Runner shows up. She emerges, a stack of files filling her arms.

'You're the eager one,' she says.

My sensors detect a more upbeat mood than is normal for this time of the day. I'm quick to take advantage. 'We need to talk. It's urgent.'

"Urgent", however, bears no weight. "Urgent" is in her DNA. Nonetheless, she doesn't try to put me off. Another positive.

Five minutes later, coffee poured, a cardboard tray of muffins unwrapped, she's geared up and ready. I turn off my phone.

'It better be good.' With a half-smile.

By now I've learned to ignore the jabs. 'Okay, straight to the point. All the cops had were twenty pages of Lyle's script, the same twenty pages you would have seen . . .'

Etcetera, etcetera, until I get to the Lyle-Aubrey link. 'So the play Lyle was writing was based on Aubrey's death, which happened on a stretch of beach that's what . . . half a kilometre from where we're sitting.'

The muffin is getting harder for her to swallow.

I don't stop. 'And which Lyle figured wasn't a straight-forward drowning.'

She washes it down with coffee. 'You're kidding me. Not another murder? In the name of God . . .'

'Forty years apart.'

'Rising Tide—sitting on a bloody hotbed of homicide.'

I'm not sure I would put it that way. But then again, I don't have her creative mind.

'The drowning—so Lyle never mentioned it?'

She shakes her head. Not what I was hoping for.

'Nothing rings a bell? Ever hear anyone talk about it?'

Head still shaking. 'Which doesn't mean it didn't happen.'

Which is not exactly advancing the investigation.

'You said the family was only here that one year. Think about it,' she says. 'They tried to distance themselves from all the torment. Went off to God knows where. Permanently took themselves out of the picture. Put Trinity as far behind them as they could.' She takes a breath. 'I don't know about you, but to me that explains why it wasn't talked about much.'

Her point made, she's deserving of a second muffin.

I need a sustaining pause myself. Preparation for an attempt to rein in her logic.

'Don't you think Aubrey would have made friends?'

'Possibly. Depends.'

'On what exactly?'

'Could have been a weird kid nobody liked.'

'I was a teacher for years. Can't say I ever taught a kid that didn't have a least one friend.'

'Then your job is to find him.'

Short and almost sweet. She's smiling in a way that says *isn't this what I hired you for?*

We've reached an end point. 'Any suggestions where to start?'

'God only knows.' She thinks about it. Eventually she points an index finger over her head. 'Try upstairs.'

Still smiling. Is that the best she can do? 'My faith is not that strong.'

She erupts in laughter, controlling it only long enough to insert, 'The costume department.' And then, 'Those three women have lived here all their lives.' Eventually she manages, 'You didn't think I meant . . .'

I laugh it off, but it's no match for her guffaws.

She's been put through the wringer this summer, yet retained her sense of humour. A good thing, if you want to look at it that way.

Donna turns out to be right. With the visit to the costume department I strike pay dirt.

Yes, they remember Rev. Mercer. 'He was a very good preacher. Lovely speaking voice,' says the oldest of the three.

Yes, and such a shame what happened that night on Tarpin's Point. 'Poor Mrs. Mercer. A mother would never get over something like that.'

And Aubrey. 'Drugs. The devil take the drugs is all I got to say.'

But for Lisa, the youngest of the three women, that isn't all.

She stands behind an ironing board, pressing a pair of newly altered pirate pantaloons. 'Always one, every season. Keeps piling on the weight over the summer and by the time the last *Pageant* rolls around, no way can he fit into his costume. Not that I'm complaining. More work for us.'

She does, eventually, get to my question. 'Aubrey was two grades ahead of me.'

I'm careful not to be putting words in her mouth. 'Aubrey had friends, people he hung around with?'

Lisa sets the iron upright. 'He was the minister's son, so it wasn't easy. The boys gave him a hard time. Called him "choir boy" to get under his skin.'

'Fights?'

'Not that I remember. He drank and smoked up, a lot, trying to prove he was one of them.'

'The devil take the drugs.' The echo from behind us.

'It wasn't all about the beer and the dope. He studied and got good marks. He set his mind on getting through the year. Once that summer was over he'd be gone. Off to university and that would be it. He wouldn't have to put up with the trouble-makers anymore.'

'What about the night he drowned?'

'I wasn't there. I can't tell you much.' She's back to ironing.

'The RCMP figured he wandered into the water drunk and got into trouble.'

She hesitates. 'Some of us weren't so sure. Doesn't entirely make sense if you think about it. The water would have been like ice that time of the year.'

'So high he didn't feel a thing if you ask me. The devil . . .'

Yes, the cursed drugs. In any case, too simple an explanation.

'How would I find out who was in his class?'

Lisa uprights the iron again. 'I remember some, but I wouldn't be able to list them all. I wonder if Mom still has my old school yearbooks. I packed up all that stuff years ago. They might be somewhere in her basement, if she hasn't thrown them out by now.'

Hadn't thought of that. Graduating Class pictures. Names. Nicknames. Pet Peeves. Ambition. Probable Fate. And God only knows what other investigative tidbits a yearbook might reveal. She promises to drop by her mother's on her way home from work.

Another cylinder just kicked in. I'm fired up. I'll check back first thing in the morning. 'Enjoy your day, folks. In case anyone's wondering, I gave up the demon weed long ago.'

It's meant to be a joke. It falls pretty flat, except for the half-smile from behind the ironing board.

I meet up with the young man and dog just outside the theatre. On the way to the car I turn my phone back on. A text came in a while I was in the costume department. From Randy, who was still in bed when we left the house.

Found something. Leaving it on the kitchen counter. Jess picking me up at noon.

No idea what the something could be. I check the time. 11:51. With luck Randy might still be there when we get back.

I turn to Nick. 'Where did you guys walk?'

'Out to that beach again.'

I'm not surprised. Nick is eyes and ears into this. He'd love to do his old man one better and come up with something I hadn't thought of.

'Ever think it might have been suicide?' he says.

'Possible.'

'But unlikely.'

Very professional. Inwardly, I'm smiling.

'I did some research. Right now the average seawater temperature in this part of Newfoundland is 13.6° Celsius. Do you know what it is in May?'

'Got me on that one.'

'2.3.'

'Yikes. No wonder icebergs are slow to melt.'

'As you have been known to say, "Cold enough to freeze the balls off a brass monkey".'

Yes, a treasured tag line from my youth, once generously shared with my son. Obviously it made a lasting impression.

'2.3° Celsius,' I repeat. 'Supports the theory that Aubrey didn't venture into the water of his own free will.'

'Exactly.'

'Well done, Robin.' Deserving a high five, if I weren't driving.

'Wanna know what else I thought of?'

'Hit me.'

'We need to see the police report of the drowning.'

He's right there. Not that I hadn't thought of it already. I don't tell him that. He's enjoying the spotlight.

I'll get to tracking down the report, once I take a look at whatever it is that Randy is so keen for me to see. I pull into the driveway. Next to Jess's car. Good, Randy is still here.

Just as we shut the car doors Jess tears out of the house. Terror in her eyes, panic in her breath. 'Randy . . . I found Randy passed out on the floor. I can't wake him!'

Not drunk or wrecked this time of the day. He texted me only an hour ago. I run into the house ahead of her. Randy is slumped on the floor next to the kitchen table.

Toppled from the chair he was sitting in. Puked after he struck the floor. Looking godawful.

'He's breathing,' Jess tells us. It quells our worst fear.

With Nick's help I manage to drag him clear of the table. Onto his back. Basic first aid comes flooding back.

Pulse—fainter than normal but definitely there. Breathing—shallow, quick, but now near hyperventilation.

'We need to get him to the hospital. Nick, run across the road. Tell Ig.'

For me it's straight into the Bacchus Manoeuvre. One arm over his head. Roll him onto his side. Other arm on the floor in front of him. Hand under cheek for good head tilt. If he pukes again, no chance he'll choke on it.

Ig rushes in. 'What happened?'

'Don't know. We need to get him to a hospital. Jess is in no state to drive.'

'He's breathing?'

'Not good,' Jess whimpers.

'Your truck, Ig. I'll deal with him in the back seat.'

Ig rushes off. He backs the truck into the driveway and reenters the house.

It's bloody awkward for the two of us to lug one hundred and seventy pounds (at least) of inertness, let alone with two others desperate to help. Finally, on the third try, we manage to heave Randy in the back seat of the pickup.

Randy appears no worse for the manoeuvre. His breathing holds.

Jess scrambles into the passenger seat and we're gone, Nick and Gaffer left standing in the driveway.

Ig knows the road. Plus his Ram Rebel TRX is bloody King Kong on wheels.

'Give 'er shit, Ig, man!'

Damn access road—more twists and turns than the bloody Swiss Alps.

Finally we're off it and on the 230. Ready to haul ass to Clarenville. All the time eyes fixed on Randy, seatbelted upright, slumped against the door.

'The cops are thick as maggots,' Ig spews. 'We get hauled over, we'll never get there.'

Not the bloody time for common sense. 'Flick on your

flashing lights! Fuck the speed limit!'

It jerks him to action, but doesn't drive him much above the speed limit. The Ram's got a shitload of horsepower. Use it for fuck's sake.

We do get there. Finally.

Jess had the foresight to call ahead to the hospital. We haul up to the emergency entrance, a gurney and two orderlies waiting. Randy is whisked through the double doors. Jess and I fumble into masks and chase after the gurney.

We get as far as the doors of the examining room before security pivots us to the waiting area. We blurt all we know to the attending doctor—he with excessively youthful eyes above his N95, an immaculate white lab coat set off by the orange tubing of his stethoscope, the chest-piece of which bears a yellow smiley face. It's unnerving. He escapes past the doors to put his training to the test.

Jess drifts away to find a washroom. With the Ram corralled in the parking lot, Ig shows up and parks himself two metres away from me.

'Pumping gastric juices,' he says decisively across the three vacant X-signed chairs. Ig knows exactly what is going on in the examining room. Given he was once friends with someone who underwent the procedure to purge his stomach of London Dock. 'One hell of a lot of overproof rum and Coke.'

If Ig's suggesting Randy overdid it on booze or drugs, I'm not buying it.

Jess returns, looking less pale, but no less nervous. Ig turns mute, a relief. We're each submerged in our own dread.

The doctor finally emerges, the smiley face stethoscope in his lab coat pocket. We're quick to our feet.

'We pumped his stomach. Could have been an overdose, but we're not sure.'

Satisfies Ig, but not the rest of us. 'No way,' says Jess. 'I came to pick him up. We were going for a swim.'

'He texted me not long before,' I tell him.

The doctor takes note but makes no deviation from his original stance. His eyes focus indulgently, his ego intact. The man still has a lot to learn.

'What did the smiley face have to say?'

'Pardon me?'

'How are his vitals?'

The eyes deepen. As does his voice. 'The patient has stabilized.'

'But not out of the woods yet, Dr. Woodruff?' Ig says, picking up on his name tag.

'Far from it.'

Add sensitivity training to his remaining course of study. Jess starts to cry. I put an arm around her and draw her close.

The doctor stiffens at this display of compassion, masked though it is, seeing it only as flouting the two-metre rule.

Yes, unreservedly by the book. I'd speculate that any relationship he himself might have had with the opposite sex has been arthritic to say the least.

'Can we see him?'

'Visitors to ICU are out of the question, as per COVID protocols. In any case he's unconscious and may remain that way for some time. He certainly wouldn't know you. Unfortunately.'

Jess's tears intensify. Best to get her out of sight of the doctor before he inflicts more damage. I supply him with my cell number, should he defy expectations and feel the need to contact me first. With a deservedly curt 'We'll be in touch,' I lead Jess away.

When we're outside the hospital, free of masks, the uncertainty sharpens. I assure Jess that the situation might not be as grave as it first appeared. It does something to calm us both.

She regains control. 'He'll pull through. He's strong.'

Ig shows up. 'Touch-and-go,' he says.

Jesus, Ig.

It's a subdued Ram ride back to Trinity. I'm in the passenger seat, but for Jess's sake, I'm not about to lock horns with Ig over Randy's condition. If I'm going to hit back, better I divert to another topic, like the fact he's still driving the bloody Ram with kid gloves.

'This rig set you back, Ig?'

Caught by surprise. The last thing he wants is for me to speculate on his bank account. 'Made a few bucks on the sale of our house in Alberta.'

I daresay he did. As compared to what he paid for a couple of houses in Trouty. I'd say he coughed up more for the Ram than he did for either one of them.

Made the big bucks in the oil boom. Back home, living on the hefty fruits of retirement. 'Glad to be back then?'

'We like it. Quiet, especially in the winter months.'

'You got your Ski-Doo and quad no doubt.'

'I like to keep busy.'

'You and a few buddies?'

He doesn't volunteer much. Keeps his focus on the road. Edges past the speed limit, but slacks back every time. He works at self-control.

'You grew up in Trouty?'

It takes a while. 'Not really.'

At which point you assume the person would chime in with where exactly he did grow up. Ig leaves a gap.

'Trinity,' he says finally.

Really? 'Why didn't you buy a place in Trinity?'

'Looked at a few. Didn't find anything we liked.'

Everyone knows houses sell for a lot more in Trinity. Might have had to scale back on the Ram.

Trinity, I'm thinking. 'Growing up, did you happen to know a fellow by the name of Aubrey Mercer?'

Takes a while, but it appears to ring some sort of bell.

'Not really. He was only in school for a year.'

'Before he drowned you mean.'

He's surprised. 'A big shock for everyone.'

'You knew he was Lyle's cousin?'

He looks my way. 'I had no idea.'

'Lyle figured there was more to the story, that it was unlikely Aubrey went into the water by choice.'

A grimace takes over his face. 'Lyle figured someone forced him into that water? You got to be kidding.'

'Apparently that was his theory.'

'Everybody had a theory.'

Obviously, it was all the talk back then. 'What's yours?'

'Aub was a strange bird. Brains to burn but no common sense. He'd do anything on a dare just to prove he wasn't chickenshit. It was cold as hell but the idiot was too stoned to care. But by the time he got up the nerve to go in the water it was daylight and everyone else had buggered off. Nobody saw it. Guess all you want, but there was fuck all anybody knew about how he got in trouble.'

I take time to get my head around it. For someone who didn't really know him, Ig sure has a definite opinion. 'Who's "everyone else"?'

'You know, the crowd around the fire.'

'You were there, Ig?'

'Left early. Girlfriend wanted to go.' He looks over at me with a trace of a smile. 'You know.' His hand gripping the steering wheel rubbing back and forth. Exciting the Ram.

Ig, horny teenager, needing to get his rocks off before he calls it a night. Hard to picture, given how time has worked him over since then, but I give him the benefit of the doubt.

By the time the postcoital Ram exhales in its driveway in Trouty, I have a fresh view of Ig.

Ig the tactless, well-off retiree maybe has a theory with some merit. Maybe Lyle got it all wrong.

Ig strides off to meet an anxious wife. I retrieve my cellphone and slow down as we cross the road. Jess heads into the house. I lean against my smaller, well-aged vehicle and blow out a lungful of tension.

And just maybe Lyle's murder had nothing to do with Aubrey and I've set myself on a pointless chase to a dead end. Wasted my time and Donna's trust. Not to mention her money.

'Donna.'

I'm surprised she answered the phone. 'It's Sebastian.'

'Can you make it quick. I'm late for a meeting.'

'Randy's in the hospital.'

'Good God, now what?'

I go straight to what I know, which leaves a hell of a lot I don't know. She's desperate for reassurance that he's going to be all right. Something I can't give her.

'Tell me it's not attempted murder,' she says. 'Tell me there's not a goddamn lunatic on the loose, driving another nail in the coffin of Rising Tide.'

'I'm pretty sure it's not.'

'Pretty sure? That's not what I need right now, Sebastian.'

I have no worthwhile comeback.

I slip the cellphone back in my pocket and lean against the car. The energy I need to tackle this new snarl in the investigation is fighting to show itself. It will. Give it time. You're still new at this game, Sebastian. Give it bloody time.

The cell rings.

I stare at the caller ID.

'Sebastian, are you there?'

'Sorry. Yeah, I am.' I revive my cool. 'Ailsa, hi.'

'I'm at Goobies.'

'Having a few words with Morris the Moose?' It's all that comes to me.

There's a pause at the other end.

Morris, moose statue, in Goobies. Long-standing tourist attraction. There's comfort in knowing the sense of humour survived, misplaced though it is. I take a deep breath.

The pause stretches on. 'Sorry.'

'I'll be out your way before long. We need to meet up.'

To compare notes, one assumes. I give her directions to the house in Trouty.

I focus on making the transition to what happened to Randy. I sense she's taking mental notes. 'Doctor thinks he may have overdosed,' I tell her. 'I'm not so sure. I suggest that when you reach Clarenville, you stop at the hospital and assess the situation.'

'Thank you, Sebastian.' Still a slight whiff of an upper hand? She adds, 'We'll talk it over.'

'You and the cops in Clarenville?'

'That, too. No, I mean Inspector Olsen. He's been helping out.'

Somewhat bemused. More bewildered.

'I asked him to come along.'

She needs to add "for the ride".

I refrain from asking what special talent Frederick Olsen brings to the investigation, what warrants bringing along the RNC when, one assumes, the RCMP is more than capable of going it alone.

'Inspector Olsen has been looking more deeply into the agricultural component of the plant evidence.'

What? What "agricultural component" of what "plant evidence"? What the frig is she talking about? What exactly is he doing? Drawing on his experience of sowing wild oats?

I should be beyond such a quip, unvoiced though it is. I've moved on from Olsen's partnership with my ex. I have. Since Ailsa entered the picture, I definitely have.

And now, with Olsen showing up, here I am suddenly thinking of him as a third wheel. Granted, I'm being nothing if not optimistic.

'I should go,' Ailsa says. 'We'll see you late this afternoon.'

Yes they will. 'I'll make supper. Give Morris my best.'

You'd think I'd welcome reinforcements. I do, in one sense, the common one.

But not in the sense that I don't have much in the way of new leads, nothing that would impress Inspector Bowmore. I had hopes pinned on whatever it was that Randy was referring to in his text, but that proves a dead end. Neither Jess nor Nick has seen anything. Nothing on the counter, not even dirty dishes, nothing uncovered in a search of the rest of the house that could possibly be it.

The whereabouts of the unknown object resurfaces a couple of hours later, after Jess has left and the RCMP/RNC combo arrive. One of several topics of conversation between mouthfuls of pan-fried cod.

Nothing better than fresh cod fried in rendered pork fat. Temperature and timing spot on. Cooked, not overcooked. Fork friendly, breaking apart in thick, succulent flakes.

'Well done, Nick. Well done, Sebastian.' At least something I do is impressive.

It is a complement to promising news on the Randy front. The inspectors spoke to Dr. Smiley Face at the hospital in Clarenville and Randy appears to be out of danger. All his vitals have improved and seemingly it's only a matter of time before he regains consciousness. A huge relief.

Nick and I have given them the lowdown on the discovery

of the collapsed Randy. Ailsa pushes deeper. Did we notice if there was anything on the table? A coffee cup perhaps? Food of any kind?

'Don't know for certain. I ran straight for Randy. I seem to recall something. Not sure what, to be honest. Dishes maybe.' Not much help. Glaring lack of instinct for observation on my part.

So over to Nick. He, of course, was left in the house after we set off for the hospital. Nick pushes back from the table, walks to the kitchen counter and retrieves something from the cupboard above it. Two Stella Artois beer cans, encased in plastic wrap. He places them in the centre of the table.

'Exhibits A and B.'

I ask the obvious question. 'What is this?'

'There was nothing on the table,' Nick announces, 'but there were two beer cans overturned in the kitchen sink.'

'Randy liked his beer,' I inject. 'Apparently any time of the day.'

Nick heightens the drama. 'I have preserved the surface areas, in case there is a need to check for fingerprints. The plastic also prevents evaporation of any traces of liquid that have might have remained inside.'

What's with this kid?

'Well done,' Frederick pronounces, as if it is not obvious to everyone.

And where do you think he learned the importance of preserving evidence? If it is evidence. Of what?

'Randy's stomach contents are being analyzed as we speak,' notes Frederick.

Now there's a pleasant image to complement the cod.

'I've requested the lab put a rush on it,' he adds, in an unnecessary display of his importance to the investigation. 'I'll get them to have a look at the beer cans as well.'

Nick retakes his seat. Followed by an exchange of smiles between him and (should his mother continue down the path on which she's barrelling) a future stepfather. I am not impressed. I am somewhat pissed to be exact. He had plenty of opportunity before the others showed up to let me in on his antics with the beer cans. I glance at Nick, unsmiling. He glances back, his sudden shine dulled.

Okay, I'm not being fair to the kid. I'm being something of a petulant ass. But I'm not about to override what's in my mind, not when it comes to my son.

The meal was bound to be awkward—Nick sitting down at a dinner table with the both of us, the two men on the opposite side of the custody arrangement. But it had to happen sometime. Just piss-poor timing.

Frederick senses it. Ailsa, too, can tell something is up.

'So, Inspectors, we're possibly thinking more foul play?' My pronounced enthusiasm lands with a thud. But it does abruptly disrupt their focus. As well as offsetting the uninspired sliced banana and ice cream that is dessert.

An uncomfortable Nick suggests he take Gaffer for a walk, which I'm a bit quick to endorse.

'We'll need to see the results of the lab tests,' says Ailsa unnecessarily, once he is out the door. 'And interview Randy when he's able to talk.'

With just the three of us, there's a jockeying for position. I'm determined not to be intimidated by the two uniforms opposite me. This is the point at which I pick up the deck and begin laying my cards on the table. 'Let's assume for the moment that Randy ingested something that had the potential of poisoning him. We'll start with the obvious—is suicide a possibility? Based on what I've seen of Randy over the time I've been here, which is quite a bit considering we live in the same house, I would rule that out. But which leads to more questions. How did the poison get in the beer, if in fact it *was* in the beer? And, more importantly, why? And how is that related to the missing object he might or might not have left on the counter?'

I note their lack of response. To be expected, given their ingrained need for lead positions.

I press on. 'And how might that object be related to the poisoning of Lyle? And how did it go missing?'

'Backtrack for a minute,' says Olsen. 'Did Randy and Lyle get along? Could Randy have had a motive for getting rid of Lyle? Maybe he's been outplaying you, Sebastian, planting false leads to put you off the scent.'

'Like poisoning himself? C'mon.'

The curt dismissal doesn't go over well.

Even so, I can't resist. 'So he takes just enough to do a job on himself, but not quite enough to make it permanent?'

'It's possible. Stranger things have happened.' Ailsa to the rescue. 'I learned a long time ago that you don't dismiss anything out of hand. The criminal mind is often far from logical.'

Now, there's one worth quoting, should I ever find myself in need of such an all-around pithy comeback.

Time to lay down a few more cards.

'The manuscript you sent, Ailsa, of the play Lyle was writing . . . turns out it was about a cousin of his who lived in Trinity, and who drowned under mysterious circumstances.'

It cements their attention, up to a point. 'When was that?' she asks.

'In the 1970s.'

'You mean fifty years ago?'

'Closer to forty.'

No change in what's starting to look like skepticism. 'What's the connection?'

'Not sure at this point. I'm waiting to get my hands on the

cousin's school yearbook.'

'I see.'

Thud. No longer sounding like a potential ace up my sleeve.

'Good luck with it,' adds Olsen.

Fine. Play the battle-scarred cop who's been around the block more times than he cares to remember. See if I'm impressed.

'Thanks for supper,' says Olsen, getting to his feet. 'Nothing like fresh cod.'

Spare me.

They head towards their rather underwhelming cop car. I look across the road, hoping the beastly black Ram is there so I could point out the vehicle option recently made available to the lowly PI. The driveway is empty, unfortunately.

'I'll be in touch,' says Ailsa, with a scrap more warmth than expected. She smiles and takes the driver's seat. Good to see Olsen wane into second place.

I'm cleaning up from supper when Nick and Gaffer reappear. Nick goes straight to the kitchen sink, without a word, without a look in my direction. He runs water and squirts in detergent.

'So, how was the walk?'

'Sorry about what happened.'

'No need.'

'Sorry I pissed you off.'

Reads me like a book. 'It's okay.'

'I don't like Fred all that much. Not really.'

'I'm sure you don't.'

'Not by a long shot.'

It's not what he's said, it's how hard he's trying.

That's good. I keep the satisfaction to myself. 'Give me a hug and we'll call it square.'

And when he does, how can I not take a handful of suds from the sink and plaster it against the back of his neck.

Of course he's going to fight back. Of course he's going to fill both his hands with suds and come after me, sending Gaffer into a barking frenzy.

'Dickhead' he calls me, hoping I'll launch a counterattack.

Not tonight. Not with all that's happened today, with so much uncertainty still. I haven't got the energy. I just stand and smile.

Nevertheless there's a lot to be said for eventually polishing off what's left of the Lagavulin.

SCENE 2

LABOUR DAY WEEKEND is here. One final smack at the *Pageant*. My last reincarnation of Solomon Noddy.

There's great news on the Randy front. He's stabilized and has opened his eyes momentarily. Jess has been told that the doctor expects Randy will be up to receiving visitors by tomorrow.

Even with another cast member out of the picture, Donna is determined the performance schedule will hold together. The word is she'd reenlisted the same backstage crewman and is about to reshape him into Randy's roles. She's determined that the season will go out on a high note. Another crisis outplayed. Good on her.

I manage to intercept her long enough to give her quick notice that the inspector duo are in town. 'They'll want to meet with you.'

'They've outgunned you on that one, Sebastian,' she says, chuckling. 'Meeting is all set. We'll have plenty of time after the *Pageant*.'

I see. Plenty of time. Cops open doors. And bloody wide at that.

'I thought about asking them if you could sit in on it,

but maybe not. I'm thinking it might be a distraction.'

A distraction. How gentle of her. I'll have her know that my skin has thickened considerably since I was hired by her theatre company.

A slick counterpunch is in order. 'Sorry to cut it short. I have forensics that need my attention. Before I take off, however, let me offer a suggestion. If you haven't already done so, read up on myclobutanil.'

I smile and leave her standing there, arms still folded.

Forensics, as I said, in the broad sense of the term.

After I submitted an online form (compliments of the Access to Information Act) and badgered a reluctant Sergeant Simmons, a scan of the RCMP report of Aubrey's drowning was finally dusted off and grudgingly directed to my inbox. Nick and Gaffer follow me to a secluded outdoor spot around the back of the theatre, well out of any possible sighting by Donna, but still within range of her Wi-Fi. Nick is as gung-ho as I am to see if it leads anywhere. All eyes focus on the screen.

RCMP officers reported that "a total of fourteen young adults" were interviewed (including, I note, Ignatius Payne), several of whom (Ig not among them) "admitted to underage consumption of alcohol." No mention of weed. All had similar stories. That Aubrey remained at the fire, and was certainly alive, if inebriated, when they left. An autopsy was performed.

"Death by drowning" according to the autopsy, with no visible injuries to the deceased. "Temperature shock likely played a part. No foul play is suspected."

It is short and seemingly conclusive. Nothing we didn't expect. There is one addendum: "Some individuals interviewed have plans to depart for employment opportunities in mainland Canada. All individuals interviewed were instructed to supply contact information, updated as needed, for a period of two years."

Bummer. We both had hopes pinned on finding something, anything that might catch our collective eyes as being out of place. Gaffer senses our frustration, and in lieu of swearing, issues several sharp yelps.

I slip my phone back in my pocket. There's still the yearbook, if it comes through.

'Good reception, b'ys? Wi-Fi keeping you busy?'

It's Donna, peering through the alders from the road above. Not so secluded after all. Must have been the damn yelping.

'Just practising lines for the *Pageant*.'

'Sure you are.'

No recourse but to move off, out of her line of sight and clear of the theatre. Fighting the angle of the tail between the damn legs.

Getting to the Costume Department will have to wait until the *Pageant* is over.

Which is not soon enough. I do my successive bits, making sure I don't screw up the last show of the season, although my mind is elsewhere, not helped by the sight of plain-clothed Bowmore and Olsen trying to look inconspicuous in the crowd. Just what the frig are they up to? Got their cop antennae trained on someone in the cast?

Nick, unlike his father, thinks it's all great, determined to take his sideshow up a notch. No doubt for the benefit of the inspectors, though more for Donna. To quote the future star before the show began, 'I'm out to nail this one. Make sure I'm permanently on her radar.' Can you believe it? He'll be weeks back in St. John's before he falls back down to earth.

The final scene ends, mercifully. Straightaway I'm on the move, while Nick and Gaffer head off to the theatre dressing room to shed their costumes for the last time.

Lisa has been expecting me, since this morning. Though not in pantaloons and jerkin.

'I was in a hurry.' But not the time to get sidetracked. 'Any luck?'

She's smiling. All bets are on.

Lisa fishes the yearbook from one of those handmade, elaborately quilted tote bags favoured by outport women. She clears a spot on her ironing board and sets it down. Then takes a Lysol Disinfecting Wipe and gives it a quick once-over front and back.

'Have a look,' she says, standing back.

I approach the book with trepidation.

There's a lot riding on this one thin, cheaply produced volume.

My status in the investigation for one thing, in the brilliant blue eyes of one Ailsa Bowmore. To say nothing of the balding Olsen.

I force all that to the back burner. I'm banking on the book holding some lead into who might have played a role in the drowning of Aubrey, and just maybe the poisoning of Lyle, and, you never know, the near miss of Randy.

A tall order. I eagerly anticipate the plunge into the pages as I open Lisa's school yearbook for 1978–79. In my early life in the classroom I was more than a few times the teacher advisor to the yearbook committee. In those days the whole book was put together from a kit, shipped off, printed, and weeks later, multiple boxes of yearbooks showed up, in time for distribution before graduation and the end of the school year.

I flick past the dedication, past the intro from the yearbook committee, past the principal's message, past the unconvincing smiles of the teaching staff. Straight to the individual photos of the graduating class, four to a page, each with their own Character Quote, Ambition, Probable Fate, Weakness, Pet Peeve, Character Song, Nickname, and Pet Saying.

Possibly a treasure trove. And there he is, halfway through

the alphabet, Aubrey Mercer. I lift up the book from the ironing board for closer inspection.

Character Quote: Silence is as deep as eternity; speech is as
shallow as time.

Takes a while to sink in. Some grads would have made up
their own, others picked something from the endless list that
came with the kit.

'Find a seat, sit down.' Lisa tells me. 'There's no rush.'

I settle in next to a vacant sewing machine, eyes fixed on the
photo of Aubrey. Juxtaposed against my memory of the photo
I saw in Keels, and Aubrey starts looking like a long-haired
version of Lyle.

Ambition: Psychiatrist. *Probable Fate:* Psycho.

Weakness: 12 Elan, Bowie. *Character Song:* Two For
The Show. *Pet Peeve:* soggy French fries, I.C.P.

Nickname: Aub, Choir Boy. *Pet Saying:* Up yours!

All ripe for interpretation. But tough to figure out, exactly.
The yearbook committee would have come up with some of
these choices for each person in the graduating class, but would
likely have run it by them before it went to print. Maybe not.
I switch back to the photo of the yearbook committee to see if
Aubrey happened to be on it. He wasn't.

I remember that grads were pretty loose about what went in
the yearbook, given that they'd soon see the last of high school,
and all the personal crap that went with it. I suspected some of
them used it as a way to get back at anyone who had been a
particular pain in the ass.

Aubrey could have been someone fighting back from being
dumped on. Then again, what kid decides he wants to be a
psychiatrist? Maybe it was a joke. And "psycho"? Not sure how
seriously I should take that either.

Ski-Doo's 12 Elan. No surprise there. Every young fellow in
the outports would have had a snowmobile in winter. Even if

it was the old workhorse Elan and not some spiffy speed demon.

He liked Bowie, probably bucking his peer group on that one. *Two For The Show*—the darker side of Trooper if I remember correctly.

I.C.P.? I haven't a clue.

'Any idea what this stands for?'

Lisa peers over my shoulder to where my finger is pointed. 'Odd there's three, but maybe someone's initials?'

'You mean a classmate?'

'Could be. Could be some girl who dumped him. Could be code for something.'

I scout ahead, to what turns out to be the only "P" in the class.

Payne. 'Fuck.'

I look around the room at three disapproving faces.

'Sorry about that.' Back to the book, 'Ignatius Conan Payne.'

Lisa chuckles. 'Of course.' Still chuckling. 'What in heaven's name were his parents thinking when they named him?'

'You never know.' Speaking from experience.

In fact, of course, I do know. Ig told me. He just didn't add the fact that his father also threw in Conan for good luck. 'Ig Conan Payne.' I have to smile.

'Iggy. Everyone called him Iggy back then. You know, like Iggy Pop.'

The Godfather of Punk. Iggy Pop, Iggy Payne. Way too much.

'Or Conan the Barbarian. When he was being a real pain in the butt.'

'He and Aubrey didn't get along, I take it?'

'He drove Aub crazy. Did all he could to get under his skin.'

'Didn't the guy fight back?'

'He had the quick putdown, you know, pretty sharp with his tongue. He was also smart enough to know that if it came to a fight Iggy would have beat the crap out of him.'

'A royal pain, in other words.'

'He'd say he was only doing it for fun. He had his friends, like Alan Duffett, just as bad as he was. But, you know what it's like. Nobody's all bad.'

I do know. Single class per grade, the students together since kindergarten, so by high school they've generally learned to get along. Being a continuous asshole doesn't play in one's favour.

'He was worse when he had a few beer. And Aub not being from here didn't help. He hadn't made enough friends to back him up, especially after the girlfriend incident.'

My eyes widen. Lisa doesn't need a prompt.

'Stephanie. She found something to like in Ig, I guess, but it looked to me she wasn't, you know, crazy, crazy about him. Anyway, they had a fight about a month before graduation and broke up. And the night after it happened Aub decides to ask her to be his date for the grad.'

'Let me guess. Ig blows a gasket and smacks him one.'

'That was pretty much it. But fortunately, no permanent damage,' Lisa tells me. 'So, anyway, Iggy and Steph make up and Aub ends up going to the grad by himself.'

'You think that was the end of it as far as Ig was concerned?'

'Who knows? You'll have to ask him.'

She's right. I need to go straight to the horse's mouth. As it is, it's far from my only question. Like why, when we were driving back from the hospital, didn't he say he and Aubrey were in the same graduating class? I can see maybe not saying much about all the shit that went on between them, but why downplay the fact he knew him?

'Or talk to Steph,' Lisa adds. 'She eventually chased Ig to Alberta. They ended up married, and she stuck with him, which surprised a lot of people to be honest. Though, apparently, it got pretty rocky. From what I heard she never liked Alberta. And now, finally, after all these years, she got her way.'

Back home. Ig's "missus" whom I've never seen.

Lisa goes back to her work. 'Borrow the yearbook if you want,' she says.

'Really?'

'Disinfect it before you give it back.' She's smiling.

Me, too. 'Perfect. Thanks.'

I take a last look at Ignatius Conan Payne, before closing the book and tucking it under my arm.

Character Quote: Some people break their neck to study, I break my studying to neck.

Ambition: Electrician. *Probable Fate:* Electrocution.

Weakness: "Stephie", Arctic Cat. *Character Song:* Taking Care Of Business. *Pet Peeve:* A.M., no snow.

Nickname: Conan (the Barbarian), Iggy Piggy.

Pet Saying: Slouzo!!

'To neck.' Nick says. 'What does that mean?'

'Are you serious?' We're on our way back to Trouty. Nick, of course, is all eyes when I show him the yearbook.

He doesn't know what necking is. And I was worried he was growing up too quickly. This is good.

I break it to him gently. 'It means to kiss someone, like on the neck. It's called necking.'

'You mean like making out without all the heavy breathing? Before they get to the good stuff.'

Miscalculated. 'You could say that.'

'So that's what you guys called it. Back in the day. Interesting. Someone should compile a dictionary of ancient sex slang.'

'Let's stop there, shall we.'

An opportune time to drop in the convenience store and

pick up something for supper. Spare myself the extra insight into what currently circulates in teenage minds. I have more than enough to deal with at the moment.

'I've been thinking,' says Nick, when I hop back in the car. He closes the yearbook and wedges it between the seats, 'It could all be a lot of BS. Guys like to sound tough, but that's not always who they really are. I can't picture Ig as a bully, can you?'

'In other words, assholes don't necessarily stay assholes all their lives.'

'I say talk to Ig. Tell it to him straight. See what he says.'

Which could mean I'm barking up the wrong tree. Again.

There is another, more intense prospect on which to pin my hopes. I text Jess before pulling out of the parking lot. 'Any word on Randy?'

We're just outside Trouty when the phone dings. Nick checks it for me. 'She says he's awake, but confused. She says she's been given the okay to visit him in the morning.'

'Yes. Good on ya, Randy. Tell Jess I'll go with her. Tell her I can pick her up on the way.'

I'm thinking, if Dr. Smiley Face has settled down, I might get a few words with Randy myself. One step ahead of the cops. Before they show up and have their go at him.

As we pull into the driveway, I see that the Ram is gone again. Needs its exercise I guess, so it won't seize up.

'Turn the oven on 375,' I tell Nick. 'I'll be right in. Just want to check if Ig will be back soon.'

I'm also anxious to meet Stephanie finally. A short ring of the doorbell.

I wait a while. Maybe she and Ig have gone off together. I'm just about to ring a second time when the door eases open.

It's obvious the woman has been crying.

'I'm Sebastian, Ig's friend from across the road. Is something wrong? Can I help?'

She leans against the door frame and inhales deeply, in an attempt to regain control of her emotions.

'Did something happen to Ig? Did he have an accident?'

She shakes her head. She's wearing leggings and a thin sweater over a tank top. Had she not been so distraught, I might have thought I had interrupted a yoga session. She's sure not the plain, thickset housewife that "missus" led me to expect.

'I need to talk to you.'

It's an invitation inside, though it seems more out of necessity than goodwill.

She leads the way to the kitchen. It looks to have recently undergone an expensive makeover. Granite countertop, heavy duty gas range, sleek grey cabinets. With an island in the centre and two stools on opposite sides.

'Cappuccino?'

Yes, definitely not the rural housewife. She efficiently sets the Italian-looking machine in motion, while carefully placing a small plate of biscotti next to me. 'I made them myself. Dried fig and pistachio.' She makes more than tea buns, it would appear.

Her hand is shaking as she fills the cups and sets them in place on the island. She sits down and is again struggling to hold back tears.

'Ig is gone. I don't know where.'

It sets me back. 'Since when?'

'Yesterday, after he came back with you from the hospital.'

'He didn't tell you where he was going?'

'I thought you might know. Or at least have some clue.'

I take a moment to think back. 'Nothing I can pinpoint. I'm sorry.'

'He hasn't been himself for a while. He got back from the hospital with it in his mind to take off. He loaded a bunch of gear and a few supplies aboard the truck, then hitched on the boat trailer. The last I saw was him driving out the road, boat in tow. He texted me to say he'd be gone for a while, not to worry.'

'Just the one text?'

She nodded. 'I texted back. I phoned. He hasn't answered. Nothing.'

'He's never done anything like this before?'

'He goes off fishing or hunting with a few of his friends. But that's planned. Never like this, never out of the blue.'

'Maybe he picked up someone along the way.'

'I phoned around. Nobody he's gone off with before has talked to him since last week.'

'Have you searched the house for any clues to where he might have gone? Anything. Notes he might have made?'

'That wouldn't be Ig.'

'Anything left in pockets maybe?'

'I haven't looked. I tossed his dirty clothes in the hamper.'

'Worth checking.' My list of suggestions has dried up prematurely.

I follow her to the laundry room. She dumps the contents of the hamper on the floor. Some have pockets, some not. I leave the intimate task of sorting to his wife, though I can't help noticing that Ig is into colourful underwear. I had no idea you can get boxers with Budweiser emblazoned across the crotch, beer suds rimming the thighs. Who would have thought it. Confirms my opinion of the beer.

The Nike track pants appear to be our best bet. Stephanie slips her hand into each pocket. The retrieval is not promising. A wad of soiled tissues, an empty yellow M&Ms packet, a solitary screw.

The items need separation and inspection to confirm there's nothing further to be uncovered. Stephanie plants them on the top of the dryer and invites me to do the job.

Such tasks hardly befit the image of a private detective. I poke at the tissues, separating them, with negative results.

But, damn it all, the canary-yellow wrapper is a different story. What I thought was the torn-off corner of the wrapper is actually what my trained eye now recognizes as a crunched-up fragment of a canary-yellow Post-it note. That's been written on.

With my index finger I carefully iron it flat, adrenalin coursing.

"Slouse—check Ig's yearbook profile." That's what it says, in plain English. Except for "slouse", which throws me off.

Hold on. 'Wait one minute,' I tell Stephanie. I run out of the house, and across the road to the car.

Stephanie is in the kitchen when I get back. I flip through the pages of the yearbook. 'Look at that. "Slouzo!"' My impatient finger points to the last line in Iggy Conan Payne's grad profile. 'Slouse. Slouzo! Can you believe it?'

She's not sure what I believe. I'm not sure either.

'Slouzo! What does it mean?'

'I haven't heard it since high school. Only in Newfoundland, I think. Like someone falling overboard. Like smack on his back, slouzo, right into the water. There's a term for that. When a word sounds like what it means.'

'Onomatopoeia.' Ex-high-school-teacher-self kicking in.

That's beside the point. The point is water, salt water and one Aubrey Mercer drowning, perhaps thrown onto his back, slouzo, right into the water.

Am I making a direct connection between Ig and the death of his classmate Aub? I keep it to myself. If it does turn out to be the case, Stephanie will find out soon enough. If it doesn't, then no harm done. And maybe she suspects something anyway.

In any case, I quickly dig out my phone. I fire off a text to Nick.

asap see what you can find out about these two words—slouse, slouzo!

I look again at Stephanie: 'Ig used that term when he was in high school?'

'He must have. It's in the yearbook.'

'So you remember him using it. Think now.' I give it an extra something—'Slouzo!'

It seems to trigger a memory. She's turning a little red.

'You do recall him using it. Give me the context.'

She hesitates. 'It doesn't have to do with water, necessarily.'

'What do you mean?'

'Ig used it . . . like when . . . he wanted it.'

It stops my train of thought for a second. Surprised but not deterred. 'Do you mind giving me an example? I think we're on to something here with slouzo. No need to go into detail. Just how he used the word.'

'Well, like . . . slouzo, flat on his back . . . in the grass . . . naked . . .'

'I see.'

'I'm sure he used it other times. It was our secret, in a way.'

'Not after it found its way into the yearbook,' I point out, gently.

'I blame that on his buddy Alan Duffett. The little frigger was on the yearbook committee.'

It had to go back to Ig though, who couldn't keep from bragging about his sexual exploits.

As tantalizing as it is, the trail of conversation has diverged in the wrong direction. I need to stay focused, on water, not grass.

I make my departure from Stephanie, perhaps leaving her more confused than when I arrived. I try to reassure her that Ig is safe, that he's sure to be in touch soon. That he could simply be out of cellphone range.

I head back across the road to where hopefully Nick has done due diligence in the matter of the crucial pair of words.

'Have a look at this!' he says, as soon as I get in the house, forefinger planted on the page of an open book. 'Slouse. Definition: "To splash, swill or swish in or under water."'

Gold. I flip up the left side of the book to see its cover. *Dictionary of Newfoundland English.* Pure gold.

'The whole dictionary is online. That's where I found "slouse", then I remembered seeing the book around the house.'

I pick it up for a closer look. I remember it too, among a pile of books in the cabinet under the TV. I figured it belonged to Randy, or had been left there by someone else who rented the house.

'I found it on the arm of the couch when I was cleaning up after you guys took Randy to the hospital. I put it back in the cabinet.'

So probably it did belong to Randy.

I flip through the pages, and just when I'm about to close it my eye catches a blank Post-it note stuck to the inside back cover—canary yellow and not complete. A strip has been torn from one side. I quickly retrieve the bit recovered from Ig's pocket and place it next to the torn edge. Carefully adjusted, and it's an exact match!

I spew an explanation to Nick. No attempt to tame my excitement.

'Wow,' says Nick. 'So what are you thinking?'

'That the book belonged to Lyle. A reference book for a writer. A writer working on a play set in Newfoundland. Looked up "slouzo", only came up with "slouse". But un-doubtedly connected. A local dialectic variation that he figured connected Ig to the drowning!'

'Holy shit, we're good!' says Nick. Gaffer yelps his en-dorsement.

'Okay, okay. Now what?'

Rhetorical question.

'You and Gaffer hold the fort. Text me if there are any new developments. I gotta get back to Trinity right away.'

I'm out the door, and now that I know the road well, I'm at the parking lot of Rising Tide in just over eight minutes.

I hurry inside and straight for Donna's office. I come to a standstill in the doorway to find her with Ailsa and Olsen, all three of them standing maskless and deadly serious. It appears their meeting is just breaking up.

I'm tempted to check the time on my phone. I'll save myself the exact measure of resentment. At least an hour and a half's worth.

I dispense with the mask. Join the impromptu bubble. 'You had lots to talk about I see.'

It's an intrusion, welcomed or unwelcomed. I'm not about to give them any opportunity to reveal which it is. I unload the school yearbook and the *Dictionary of Newfoundland English* on the closest thing I can find to a vacant spot on a flat surface.

'Have a go at this. Believe me, it will be worth it.'

I open the books to the appropriate pages. It only takes a couple of minutes of explanation. Straightforward and smack on the point. 'Ig has flown the coop. To where? His wife has no idea. If that's not a sign of guilt, nothing is.'

Momentary stunned silence is not unexpected.

'Impressive,' says Ailsa, finally.

'But not exactly conclusive,' Olsen says. He glances at his partner. She, in turn, glances at me. And shrugs.

Jesus.

I turn quickly to Donna. 'You know the term "slouzo", right? You heard it before, right, living in rural Newfoundland all these years. Unlike the inspectors.' For whom, I don't add out loud, the *Dictionary of Newfoundland English* could just as well be in Swahili.

'Well, in reference to water, yes. In reference to grass, no.'
She thinks it's funny but I'll forgive that.

'See,' I say pointedly to the inspectors.

It does little to alter their apprehension. 'The problem as
I see it,' says Olsen, 'is in attempting to build a case on a little-
known word or two. It's not what I would call concrete
evidence.' He looks yet again to Ailsa for confirmation.

'It would never hold up in court, Sebastian. We need a
witness. Or at least a motive.'

'Aubrey tried to steal his girlfriend. Revenge is the first
option in the jilted lover's mind.'

'He got her back, remember,' says Olsen. 'Slouzo in the
grass.'

Deep breath, Sebastian. Control yourself. Let the nitwit
have his moment in the fucking sun.

Donna does me the courtesy of laughing again. Yes, Donna,
show whose side you're on in no uncertain terms.

'Inspectors, you don't think Randy, when he finally speaks,
will only confirm my suspicions, that Ig tried to poison him,
just as he did Lyle, and in that case succeeded, the motives
in both cases being they were getting dangerously close to
implicating Ig Payne in the death of Aubrey Mercer forty years
ago on a beach less than half a kilometre from where you're
standing?'

Olsen's eyes sweep across to Ailsa, then Donna, and back
at me. 'We'll see,' he says.

How fuckingly, pathetically patronizing. And bloody
unprofessional.

'Sebastian, we're not discounting your theory,' injects Ailsa.

How damn good of her.

She takes out a notebook. 'Ig. Short for?'

'Ignatius Payne. Dodge Ram.'

She writes. 'Trouty. I'll put out an all-detachment call. And we're seeing Randy in the morning. Plus we'll have the toxicology reports by tomorrow. In the meantime, stick with it, you never know where else it might lead.'

Grit my fucking teeth. 'Speaking of leads, what took you an hour and a half?'

The inspectors don't appreciate audacity. At this point, what the fuck odds?

Controlled bristling on Olsen's part. A trigger for Ailsa to play peacemaker. 'My sense is tomorrow will prove a turning point. Inspector Olsen and I will continue our interviews with a number of the cast.'

What's this—the detachment boys haven't been doing their job. Besides which, it's a bit late to be playing at that. 'While they're packing up to leave, theatre season over.'

Donna has been unusually quiet, up until now.

'Who knows if they'll ever be back. Who knows if there will ever be another season. Dear God, I'm counting on you two . . . I mean three . . . to solve this mess. We got to get past it, get it out of the news and move on. All this talk of murder is doing nobody any bloody good, believe me. It's killing our audience potential for next year.'

I've never seen her so emotional. She's devoted practically her whole life to this theatre company. She won't go down without a fight. But the reality is she can't do it alone. She needs us.

I step in to reassure her. 'We won't let that happen.'

Donna stares at us unrelentingly, her arms folded across her chest. 'Bloody right you won't let that happen.'

It's as if she has given the three of us a damn good collective shake. We glance at each other. Have we got it in us to set aside pride in favour of getting to the bottom of this case? I do. I don't know the fuck about Olsen.

I look straight at Ailsa, lead investigator. I give her a directional nod. We need to talk, alone. 'Excuse us for a moment.'

We exit from Donna's office to the wooden deck that connects the theatre to the path leading to Lower Gun Hill and Tabin's Point.

'I want you to follow me. It won't take long.'

She's surprised of course. And resistant.

'It's important. For Donna's sake, it's important.'

She glances at her watch. 'Frederick will be wondering . . .'

As much as I want to, I don't put the f-word before his name. 'Frederick will be fine. All I ask—this one favour.'

She doesn't say anything, just starts walking as I take the path towards the Point. It's not long before the beach comes in view and not long before we reach the grassy edge of the bank that overlooks it.

'Shall we?' I invite her to sit with me. With some reluctance she does. She's uncomfortable. She needs an explanation.

'One thing to understand about rural Newfoundland is that people generally try to get along. You might hate your neighbour's guts but you make the effort to tolerate him because nobody survives on their own. There'll always come a time when you'll need each other, whether it's helping you push your car out of a ditch or searching for your son if he gets lost in the woods. People are justifiably wary of making enemies.'

'Where's this going, Sebastian?'

I know exactly where it's going. 'In the freezing water just off this beach, Lyle's cousin Aubrey Mercer drowned. On a dark night in May, 1979.'

'I've also seen the police report.'

I press on. 'For Lyle, the question eventually became: Was it an accident, or did he drown because Ig Payne pushed him into that freezing water?'

'His conclusion?'

I can be a match for her efficiency. 'We'll never know. Unless we get to read the rest of the play, unless his laptop is found. I'd say there's zero chance of that happening.'

'You're left with a lot of unanswered questions, Sebastian. And even if you had the answers they could very well lead nowhere. In the meantime we have a murder left unsolved.'

'I have my own conclusions.'

She stares at the beach, likely pleading with herself to find a way to end this.

'Do you want to hear them?'

She turns to me. 'Your call.'

A bit harsh, Ailsa. I stiffen my response.

'First conclusion—Ig pushed him into that water.' I give her a few seconds to absorb it. 'So then the question becomes— was Ig out to kill him? Second conclusion—I doubt it very much.' Another couple of seconds. 'Give him a fright for a laugh? Probably. Not exactly an accident. But neither was it premeditated. He left him thinking he'd eventually get back on his feet, stumble out of the water and walk home.'

She's quick to come back at me. 'Okay, let me buy into that for the time being. What you're saying is that decades later Lyle comes along, starts asking questions to anybody who might know something about the drowning, gets it in his head that Ig was responsible for what happened, and decides to write a play that points the finger at him. Then Ig Payne somehow gets wind of this and sets out to put a stop to it. By poisoning Lyle. And when Randy somehow starts getting suspicious, Ig tries to do the job on him as well.'

I'll admit hearing it articulated like that, out loud and matter-of-factly, is a bit of a jolt to someone who has only ever had it swirling tentatively around in his head.

I can't be sounding indecisive. 'Basically, yes.'

'That makes you next on his list.'

In need of a smile on my part. 'You could say that.' And a need to break the tension. 'Lucky for me Ig flew the coop before Randy set you guys on his tail.'

A smile unrequited. She's still not attuned to the darker side of Newfoundland humour.

'You realize you haven't convinced me,' she says. 'Beside which it shoots a big hole in your rural neighbourliness theory.'

'All those years in Alberta took their toll.'

I wouldn't call what she offers a smile. Maybe a pinhole of hope. A slight hovering between the professional and the personal. 'Sebastian, I'll do this much. I'll support you to see where it takes us.'

First base, so to speak.

'Which means you and Inspector Olsen have theories of your own.' It goes to show that, being the practical investigator I am, I don't hold grudges.

'You could say that.'

'That you're willing to share?' If pressed I can be good at faking optimism.

A moment of hesitation, prolonged. 'I haven't told you this before.' Prolonged further. 'There was a joint found in the pocket of a jacket belonging to Lyle. Inspector Olsen had it analyzed. It had to be sent away, took a while. It was laced with myclobutanil. That was no surprise. What was a surprise is the fact that the particular strain of marijuana is not sold in Newfoundland and Labrador. For sale in several other provinces, but not here. So it had to have been brought in from outside.'

Okay. More than I expected. Let me think about this.

'So someone out to get him, someone from the mainland or who had recently travelled to the mainland, secretly slipped a couple of joints in his pocket, guessing he would smoke one?'

'That's not the only possibility of course.'

'Of course.'

'It could have been someone who had been here all along, someone he shared joints with before. Maybe they had a habit of trading pot.'

'Exactly. Another cast member, you're thinking?'

'We just went over the cast and crew list with Donna, with that new information in mind.'

'And?'

'We pinpointed three individuals to start. But we also realize the mainland connection might not be obvious.'

'Absolutely. Could have been someone who had contact with a transient worker who was back in Newfoundland during his time off.'

'Possibly. The weed had been harvested within the last few months according to the report, so a fairly recent transaction.'

'So you start with three possible suspects and see where that takes you.'

A slight error in judgment on my part. The inspector knows what she's doing.

'Inspector Olsen is confirming their contact information and housing locations with Donna.' She checks her phone. She stands up. 'I have to get back, Sebastian.'

This time she's the one in the lead. 'I take for granted that Randy is not on the list of three.'

'That would be the case.' She hesitates, seeming to debate whether to say more.

'Go ahead.'

'But Jess is.'

Sweet Jess! What are they up to? Thinking that Jess could possibly be the source of the weed that killed Lyle. That's what comes from spending hours behind a desk in St. John's and not on the ground where it all took place.

Let them waste their time. I'll put mine to better use. Over supper, I dig deeper into the yearbook with Nick, in case there are more tantalizing bits left to uncover. While lapping into homemade mac and real cheese. A small tribute to Randy, knowing he would love it, feeling sorry for him having to deal with whatever lurks on his hospital dinner plate.

We do a systematic review of each of the graduates. A motley collection, from outport metalheads to future MDs. Unruly long hair and jean jackets were mandatory for boys, longer hair and baggy tops for girls.

Only one of them takes a second look, the aforementioned pal of Ig, Alan Duffett. Here he is, in all his uninspiring glory. A kid with the hair and chain that makes him look like a John Travolta wannabe.

Character Quote: Money can't buy happiness but it can make a damn good downpayment.
Ambition: Life in the Fast Lane. *Probable Fate:* Wrecked.
Weakness: Arctic Cat. *Character Song:* The Boys In The Bright White Sports Car. *Pet Peeve:* Mustard buckets.
Nickname: Al. *Pet Saying:* Whatta ya at?

Sounds like a bit of a speed demon, but overall not much to work with, bearing in mind he was on the yearbook committee and would have vetted the profile. 'What's this "mustard buckets"?' Our one hope.

Nick, Google master, has the answer pronto. 'Ha! He obviously hated Ski-Doos.'

Leave it to a pubescent Arctic Cat fanatic to think he could belittle another guy's snowmobile by crapping on its yellow colour.

There's a knock on the door. I open it to find Stephanie standing there. 'Still no word from Ig.'

She's hoping I might know more. 'Come in.'

'The RCMP just called. Your friend I guess. I hadn't reported Ig missing.'

'I did. Just in case.'

She doesn't question it. I expect, in fact, it's a relief to her. I work past the awkwardness. 'Have a seat. I'll put on the kettle.'

Gaffer does his bit to help. Jumping up when she sits at the table, paws in her lap, pleading for her attention.

'I always wanted a dog,' she says, 'a small one. But Ig wouldn't have anything less than a German shepherd. So we never did.'

She rubs Gaffer behind his ears, now his friend for life. She notices the open yearbook.

'I'm sure we had a copy. Perhaps it got misplaced in the move.'

She has to be wondering how I came to have it. 'Belongs to a friend of Donna.' Which does nothing to explain why I would be interested in it. I have to avoid that as best I can, while at the same time prompting her for anything else that might prove useful. A fine line.

'I happened to be with her when she was looking through it. I didn't know anybody, of course, except Ig. When I saw his grad picture, with the long hair. I thought, I'll borrow it and haul it out the next time I see Ig, for a laugh.'

Not strictly true, of course. But true enough to cover my tracks.

Now for the transition. I point to the picture of Alan Duffett. 'That's the guy you mentioned, right, Ig's buddy?' It was clear from this afternoon that she wasn't fond of "the little frigger".

'He hung around Ig like . . . like Ig would say . . . ' She glances at Nick. 'Like shit to a blanket.'

Nick laughs out loud. My eyebrows constrict and his laughter wanes to something less jarring.

'Not the most likeable guy in the world?'

'I can look back on it now and think it was funny how Al wasn't much interested in having a girlfriend, how he'd rather tag along with us when he could. After high school it didn't matter anymore. We went our separate ways and we never saw him again. Ig might have kept in touch for a while, but if he did he never mentioned it to me. You know, new place, new life. High school fades pretty fast.'

'Any idea where he ended up?'

'Ig has never said. I doubt if he even knows.'

Nick has been taking it all in, turning silent in the process. Likely remembering the time his best friend Tyler started dating, leaving Nick out in the cold. Holding on to friends has been something of an issue with him.

'You and Ig hit it off, right?' I say to Nick, easing attention away from the book. 'You loved going out in the boat with him.'

'Ig turned into a bit of a redneck when he was out west,' Stephanie says, for a reason I can't quite pinpoint. 'But he's come around. Once we settled back in Newfoundland he took it easier. Different things taking up his energy. A different crowd taking up his time.'

Interesting. It's starting to look like they're a very mis-matched couple.

'The truck is a bit of a holdover. Where we lived in Alberta guys were known by their trucks. That rig of his would have made him king. Here, where none of his friends can afford one, he's suddenly looking like king shit.'

Nick's eyes widen. Stephanie continues to veer off, defying expectations. Haven't heard that particular turn of phrase in quite a while. A relic from my youth as well as hers.

I'm keen to know more about her relationship with Ig, and I get the sense that she might not be averse to opening up to me. I'd still be treading that fine line.

I catch Nick's eye. 'You think Gaffer could do with a walk?'

Gaffer clues in and barks. Together they make a quiet exit.

'He's a great kid,' I say to Stephanie, refilling each of our mugs. 'Do you have children?'

'A daughter and granddaughter in Halifax. That was some of our reason for coming back. To be closer to them.'

It doesn't sound like there's a husband in the picture. 'Do you get to see them often?'

'Before COVID we did. And now with the Atlantic Bubble we're planning to drive up next week.'

Which makes the fact of Ig taking off like he did all the stranger.

I see in her eyes she's thinking the same, eyes that are starting to tear up.

'We have our differences but we stayed together and made it work. We give each other space to do the things we want to do. You live through a lot when you have a family.' Her eyes close and she wipes her cheeks. 'We lost our boy.'

I hardly know what to say. 'I'm sorry.'

Gradually, a steadiness returns. 'A motorcycle accident. He was seventeen.'

'I can't imagine what you must have gone through.' It has to be every parent's nightmare.

'Grief brings you closer, Sebastian. It holds you together. Ig dearly loved his son.'

I nod in agreement.

'I think that's why he took so strongly to Nick. He wants to know his boy again.'

What do I say to that, to a woman I barely know? And what is there to say about the man who I have been thinking was responsible, years ago, for the death of another young man, a young man the same age as his son when he died.

If there is one thing I've discovered in this business it's that you can never predict who ends up involved in crime. Something can trigger the most easygoing, most cared-for person to strike out on the wrong side of the law. For whatever reason—quick money, infidelity, one too many drinks. Maybe just once, but that's all it takes, as much as that person might regret it later.

I think about my first time involved in a murder investigation. I think about Ivo, hired to do away with me because I knew too much. Ivo, who let himself be hired because he was desperate for money. Even though the scenario was foiled, even though Ivo swore afterwards he had no intention of seeing it through, that he was just going to take the upfront money and run, nevertheless that impulse, that single error in judgment, will follow him the rest of his life. Even though, when I dwell on it long and hard, I'm tempted to believe the guy.

'Do you think that truck of Ig's is a distraction?'

'We didn't need to be spending all that money. Custom this, custom that—he had to have it all. I don't really understand it. I put it down to men and their trucks. You know.'

I don't really. Not given how I spend my time.

'It doesn't make sense,' she says, 'for the way he drives. Have you noticed that?'

'Slow, you mean.' Like he didn't want to get where he was going. Now I'm thinking—like he would rather have seen Randy die before he got him to the hospital.

Stephanie hesitates. 'Ig has nightmares about a young man on a motorcycle, running a stop sign, getting slammed by a truck.'

I take even longer. To let that sink in. To sit there and have to recalibrate my perspective on Ig behind the wheel.

'Must be hard.' It's inadequate for how the woman unburdened herself to me. 'I'm sorry.'

She stands up to leave.

'Ig has his reasons for taking off like this,' she says. 'I wish I knew what they were.'

'Perhaps he needs time to work things through.'

'What things?'

Like her, I wish I knew. 'Time will tell,' I offer, as she steps outside. 'Have faith.'

Useless clichés—the best I can do? She's gone now. She needed someone to hug her and tell her it will all work out. That wasn't going to be me.

Does her revelation about Ig truly change anything? Is he any less likely to have caused Aubrey Mercer to drown, whether he intended to or not? Or poisoned Lyle Mercer and Randy Dicks, one of whom is dead, the other having barely escaped the same fate.

Randy's memory seems more critical than ever. Tomorrow could tell all.

I check my phone, turned off while Stephanie and I were talking.

One message. From Jess, telling me she doesn't need me to pick her up in the morning. She'll be taking her own car. She'll meet me at nine in the lobby of the hospital in Clarenville. After we see Randy, her plan is to drive directly to St. John's.

Why the rush? The theatre season is over, but I expected she'd hang around a while longer, at least until her boyfriend is discharged.

Leaving my head thick with possible scenarios of what took place between her and the pair of inspectors.

A fresh message. This one from Ailsa.

You're in luck. The truck has been located off a side road in Lower Lance Cove on Random Island. The truck was equipped with OnStar. Stolen vehicle tracking. It was found within an hour after I activated the alert. I'm about to let his wife know.

The fully loaded Ram backfired. OnStar tech. Pricey screw-up on Ig's part.

Any sign of his boat?

No.

Rather abrupt, Ailsa. *Is there more I should know?*

Negative.

Who says *negative* anymore? I can handle another *no*. A *no*, meaning there's more she doesn't want to tell me.

Where from here?

Open question at the moment.

Give me the time of day, Ailsa.

She quickly follows with another standard line. *Let's talk in the morning.*

That we will. And more intensely than she might be expecting.

Nite.

What is this? Is she too preoccupied to text two full words? Too anxious to get back to her RCMP underlings to use proper English?

I punch in *GOODNIGHT*. But *Good night* is what gets sent.

I mute the phone, take to the couch and reach for the laptop. *Lower Lance Cove, Random Island.*

Just as Google Maps does its business, Nick and Gaffer show up.

'Hey pal, big news.'

Gaffer springs onto the couch, paws on my shoulder, frenzied ear licking in full motion. I could use the affection. He eventually settles to one side of me, Nick to the other.

'Hit me.'

The kid knows more about OnStar than I do, given that it's never been an option for the class of used cars that I invest in.

'Fred told me about this guy in Mount Pearl who stole a

car with OnStar and the Constab nailed him just like that, wham-bam!'

'He said that—*wham-bam*?' Bit antiquated, even for Olsen.

'You know, super quick.'

Let's leave it at that. Nick doesn't need to know that Olsen keeps the *thank you, ma'am* half of that phrase for adult company.

Moving right along. I share the computer screen with him and there it is—Lower Lance Cove, not all that far away, one of a bunch of small communities on Random Island. Accessed by a causeway just before you get to Clarenville.

Another couple of clicks for what else I need. 99.4 kilometres from Trouty. One hour, twenty-four minutes driving time.

Which I can narrow down to an hour plus. Head off at daylight, get there by 7:30, giving me an hour before heading on to Clarenville hospital to meet Jess.

'No way are you going without me.'

'Nick, man, I don't think so. It might not be safe. Remember the last time.' Meaning the episode in the GeoCentre in St. John's when Nick and Gaffer found me bound and gagged with Gorilla Tape, the goon who did it still on the loose. The boy's not-so-understanding mother still hasn't forgiven me, regardless of the fact they likely saved my neck.

'Whataya mean, not safe? It's an abandoned truck in a gravel pit.'

I'm not sure I can argue with that. Given there was no boat, suggesting Ig launched it before he parked the truck. Reinforced by Google's sidebar photo of a rather spacious slipway in Lower Lance Cove.

'We'll see.'

'Don't try sneaking out of the house without waking me.'

Foiled before I even thought of it. Nevertheless, it's not good for the kid to be getting his own way so easily. He's going to have to put together a better argument than that. 'Give me one reason for you coming with me? Better make it good.'

'Ig.'

Boxing gloves fall to the sides. I see now I haven't been putting enough stock into just how much Nick had relished his time with Ig, how well the two of them got along.

'You're having trouble buying into this?'

He hesitates. 'I guess.'

'Perhaps I got it wrong.'

I almost begin the story of Ig losing his son. I decide not to. It would complicate things even more.

'I hope so,' he says.

He truly does. He's desperate to believe that Ig couldn't possibly have taken someone's life. To the point that he's willing to put it before any headway his father believes he's made in the case. Perhaps I could reach a point where I understand that.

'I think that's all the more reason for you not to come with me.'

'No way.'

That's his argument. The automated response.

I'm not about to counter it. I'll spare him that.

'I suppose you want Gaffer to come along, too.'

'Of course.'

At the mention of his name, Gaffer sits up, stares at us, and tilts his head in that way he does, questioning what exactly it means for him. He offers a quick, companionable yelp.

'Daylight and we're out the door.'

There it is. All said and done. No turning back.

ACT FOUR

SCENE 1

THE DRIVE TO Lower Lance Cove is (not surprisingly) quiet. Boy and dog doze while the driver debates the investigative life.

You think you're seeing the pieces inch together, a picture taking shape, a little hazy still, but getting there, when sensitive son suddenly tosses in a few extra pieces, outliers that, try as you might, you can't quite make fit.

Which means suck it up, take one for the team, and move on. There's work to be done.

The causeway spans Smith Sound, one of Newfoundland's largest inland waterways. It crosses to Random Island, which itself is roughly forty kilometres in length, and the second largest offshore island in the province. We're talking almost twice the size of Manhattan.

With twelve hundred people. Lower Lance Cove clutching eighty-five of them. No high-rises, but one hell of a lot of spruce trees and electricity poles. It feels like it's taking forever to get there. Despite slashing a good ten minutes from the Google guesstimate.

This early in the morning, I'm thinking a few fishermen, maybe.

What greets us is a cop car and its officer, looking high on Tim Hortons, primed for action. There are a couple of fishermen in their boats at the end of the wharf, undoubtedly all ears for what's going on.

'Well . . . now . . . Mr . . . Synard.' Wrong again. He's still pronouncing it as if it rhymes with *guard*. As if he's French. Which he isn't.

'Sergeant, that would be Synard. Rhymes with *innard*. As in guts.'

I expect the forced smile. And the slight widening of the nostrils.

'What brings you all the way from Trouty this morning?'

Let's get to the point. 'Inspector Bowmore informed me that the truck belonging to our neighbour Mr. Payne had been found. We're here to check it out with the intention of updating Mrs. Payne, his wife. Any sign of the boat?'

He's taken aback a bit more. The smile gives way to standard cop curtness. 'Just the trailer, hitched to the truck.'

'Where is it exactly?'

He points vaguely in the direction of the gravel road that continues along the shore.

Just as we're about to head towards it, a second cop car shows up. I expect RCMP backup. What we get is an energized Inspector Bowmore and her ever-ready teammate Inspector Olsen.

'Fred,' calls Nick, equally surprised. 'What are you doing here?'

My sentiments exactly. Given the pointed skepticism of yesterday.

Ailsa steps ahead. 'We've spoken to Randy.'

What, like when? It's barely daylight. What's with the early birds going all out to get the damn worm?

'We spent the night in Clarenville,' says Ailsa, acknowledging the subtle fury in my posture. 'We had planned to drive back to St. John's this morning.'

'Had?'

'Randy Dicks appears to have been drinking beer with Ig Payne before he fell ill.'

More than *appears*. 'Damn well knew it.'

'The toxicology report came through. His stomach contents showed traces of cyanide,' she says.

'As did one of the beer cans,' Olsen quietly adds.

Double bloody jackpot.

So, a bit chagrined, are we, Inspectors? I peer at them, squelching the urge to be smug, biting my tongue enough to let them off the hook. For the most part.

'Inspector Bowmore, back to my question of last night. Where from here?' My generous good nature finding a way through.

Olsen, out to re-establish his status, inserts himself. 'We have reason to believe the suspect has taken his boat offshore.'

What would be your first clue? The empty boat trailer? Bite your tongue any harder, Sebastian, and you'll end up with lockjaw.

'We believe there's a good chance he's on Ireland's Eye.'

That whips up my attention. 'Really?'

'We spoke to his wife this morning,' Ailsa says. 'She remembered he had gone there by boat before, several times in fact. Mostly from Trouty, but if it was windy he'd launch his boat from here because the Sound is more sheltered.'

'Ireland's Eye is an island,' Olsen adds, 'at the mouth of the Sound.'

'Google Maps is a great resource.'

'Drug bust central, back in the day,' Nick inserts out of the blue. Projecting what he sees as his rightful need to be in on the action.

Leaving both Olsen and me slack-jawed. Can never take the young bugger for granted.

'I've heard of it,' says Ailsa. 'Can't say I know much about it.'

Olsen is anxious to fill her in. He starts, but the words trail to a stop.

Drawing up to the wharf is an open speed boat. To judge by its size and the hefty Yamaha outboard clamped to the stern, it means business.

Police business, as I quickly discover. They've hired some guy and his boat in Clarenville to take the RCMP triple threat to Ireland's Eye. Make that a quadruple threat. Showing up behind us is a familiar SUV.

Emerging from it is one Corporal Watten. And, because he never leaves his detachment home without her, that all-around handsome black-and-tan canine, Siren.

Gaffer is not impressed. Gaffer's bark can be extraordinarily robust for a dog his size. As I have been known to say, the mutt's still got balls despite the fact that he's long ago been neutered. Siren could make mince of him in short order, except she is so well trained that she just peers in his direction in indifferent disbelief.

Nick grabs Gaffer up in his arms and walks away, hand clamped around the dog's disgruntled jaws. They'll have a man-to-man, not that it will do much good.

I'm quick to return to my train of thought before the canine interruption. 'It looks like you have plenty of room for a couple more. Inspectors, I don't need to justify our coming along. As you know, we've been friends with Ig Payne for some time. In fact, I would have to say very trusted friends.'

'Trusted friends?' says Olsen. 'You've known him what . . . two weeks, and suddenly you're a trusted friend who suspects him of murdering two people, and attempting to murder a third? What is this, Sebastian? Where the fuck . . . heck is it leading?'

The result: a definite blunting of the dialogue.

Unbecoming of an officer of the RNC. Only somewhat less unbecoming of the partner of my ex-wife and part-time housemate of my son. He shows zero remorse.

Ailsa, try as she might, cannot cover her irritation. Or is it disappointment? As for Simmons and Watten, they appear, if not amused, then too damn close to it.

Ailsa makes a valiant effort. 'Gentlemen.'

As a collective term, that's stretching it. She pauses before turning to me.

'Sebastian, if I'm to understand you correctly, you feel you would prove helpful to the situation. However, at this point, we have no idea what we might encounter. The suspect could be agitated and armed, in which case it would mean putting your life at risk. And as for Nick . . .'

'I'm fully prepared . . .'

She holds up a hand. 'You're not a trained officer, Sebastian.'

'That's the advantage I'm offering you. I'm not a threat to Ig. He knows that. I'm not about to confront him with an ultimatum. I'll be there to talk him down, get him to agree to meeting with us.'

She's shaking her head. 'I don't like to say it, but I think you're being naïve.'

Don't like to or not, she said it. It doesn't go over too damn well with me.

I square the account. 'In which case I'll hire a fisherman and his boat to take me there. In fact, he'll likely know how to get to Ireland's Eye better than your guy does. Including an easy spot to land a small boat, rather than the brute you hired. I won't bother to wait for you. I'll take off on my own to find Ig.'

There you go. Play the naïve card all you want. You others, chuckle to yourself while you're fucking at it.

I yell over to Nick, 'Stay where you're at. I'll be back in a minute.'

Jude the inactive fisherman is only too happy with an extra hundred bucks he hadn't counted on this morning. Not only that, he's got the requisite number of life jackets and the offer of a beer should I be interested.

I will be, once I retrieve two windbreakers from the car, then re-park and lock it up. Collect Nick and Gaffer and stride past the RCMP squad playing catch-up. I untie the painter as Jude fires up the outboard. And here I am sitting pretty next to the boy and dog as we head out of the cove, a yelping Siren in the background, who, by the sound of it, is no lover of boats.

Neither is Gaffer, but he's had the good sense to keep to a size that fits snugly in Nick's arms. Nick stokes him and allays his fears, while I twist the cap off a Dominion ale and raise the bottle in allegiance to my new good friend Jude.

How's *that* for naïve.

Love that wind in our faces. Love Jude's sure and steady hand on the tiller getting us there with the cop boat barely in sight.

I've hardly finished the beer when we round the headland at Ireland's Eye and a strikingly scenic, sheltered harbour comes into view. It's a relatively deep inlet, with a rocky, irregular shoreline, some of its indentations offering additional escape. We catch a glimpse of a boat anchored in one. A closer look confirms it belongs to Ig Payne. It is empty of anything but boat gear.

The shore gives way to an open grass- and shrub-covered field and beyond that a hillside of scruffy spruce and fir. No sign of anybody, but not a place we want to come ashore. Better we keep a distance and find our own landing spot. Jude reverses course and heads deeper into the inlet.

'What do you say, Jude, a hundred or more people lived here at one time?'

'At least,' says Jude. 'Father was one of them.'

There's an image of a thriving outport community before my eyes, now long abandoned, only a faint reminder of it left. Nick needs to know this stuff.

'If this was the 1940s we'd be looking at dozens of houses ringed around this harbour, together with wharves and fishing sheds. A school, a church, a post office.'

'Fish flakes everywhere,' Jude adds. 'Lined off with salt cod drying in the sun.'

'Babies born, couples married, others going to their grave.'

'Christmas concerts, church suppers, fiddles and accordions ringing through the kitchens and into the winter nights.'

Nick smiles, somewhat indulgently, but not without a spark of interest. Some of it will seep into his young townie mind and there'll come a time when he'll recall this moment and tell his own children. All you can do is take time to put it in their heads and hope for the best.

'Then the government comes along and pays people to move,' says Jude, standing up in the boat, hand on the tiller, scouting the shoreline. 'Promises them they'd be better off someplace where there's roads and cars and hospitals. They uprooted and left the whole works behind to founder and rot. A good many of them never got over it. My grandmother went to her grave vowing her heart was right back here where she knew she belonged.'

The backdrop to whatever situation might be brewing ahead of us. I swear by the fact that the past plays on the present. No way was Ig's choice of Ireland's Eye by chance. With that Ram and boat of his, there's a thousand and one places he could have gone. In fact there was time enough for him to get to the ferry and off Newfoundland altogether. Could even have ditched it all and rented a vehicle and be deep in the bowels of mainland Canada by now, no OnStar flashing on any cop's computer.

'Grab the anchor,' Jude tells me. His aim is to anchor us just off shore, shallow enough at the bow that we can get to the beach, but deep enough for the propeller blades not to strike bottom. 'But wait 'til I give you the word. Don't let it down yet.'

Hey Jude, I chant quietly, 'won't let it down.' Since we boarded his boat, I've been thinking there might come just the right moment.

'Shit, man, not you, too.' He does chuckle, which is good.

Not my most original line, but I'm out to show Nick that, at this point at least, I'm not particularly freaked out. Mentally, I'm in good shape. I can deal with Ig.

Keep Nick out of the picture, keep him safe, and I'll be fine confronting Ig. The fellow's not about to turn on me.

Making it to shore is an exercise in how not to get wet. I'm convinced the gap between the bow and dry land is too wide to conquer in a single leap. I'm no longer limber enough to risk making a fool of myself. Nick, on the other hand, is all confidence, having once performed the broad jump at his school's track meet.

He does it, with several inches to spare. Gaffer can afford to get wet and dutifully dog paddles to shore. Jude has a game plan, setting the beer cooler in the water ahead of the bow to act as a stepping stone.

'Don't be a fool, play it cool,' he says. A smirk sets deeply into his face. 'Don't make your world a little colder.'

From shore I give him the thumbs-up, plus the Newfoundland wink and nod. He leans over the bow and retrieves the cooler. Then secures the boat so it won't hit against any rocks, before striding ashore in thigh-length rubber boots.

'Can't just leave you fellers here. Besides I'd miss out on the action.' As he changes into hiking boots, he points to the other side of the harbour, to three Mounties, a dog, and Olsen, in that order, parading along the shoreline. Sergeant Simmons is carrying what looks to be a rifle case. And binoculars, which leave no doubt they've identified Ig's boat.

No point in trying to avoid them. Better to meet halfway and sort this out. In this case, concession being the better part of valour.

The armed and uniformed squad have us in their sights.

Preliminaries are a waste of valuable time. We're here, they're here, and there's nothing to be gained from disputing the fact that we have to work together. Get past the bruised egos and get on with it.

Besides which, they might think they have us outclassed (i.e., Siren no doubt feeding off the scent of Ig from something or other discovered in the Ram), but we have one very important component in our arsenal that's missing in theirs.

'Meet Jude. Jude's ancestors lived on Ireland's Eye. He knows this place like the back of his hand.'

'Hey, Jude.' That's Olsen. He snapped it out with a straight face. It would seem he's still so pissed off that his ironclad mind has no room for cultural references. His bull's eye focus—the mission at hand.

There's no denying Jude could prove to be of considerable help. Ailsa, obvious tactical leader of the squad, knows this, but chooses to acknowledge it with nothing other than an efficient 'Right.'

'We set the ground rules,' she says. 'Above all—caution. At this point we have no idea what we're about to encounter. The suspect might or might not be armed. His state of mind is likely volatile. He could surrender himself to us, he could make a run for it, he could attempt to do himself harm. All open questions.'

She turns to the three outliers. The unkempt squad. But, given we're not going anywhere and one of us at least might prove valuable, we're to be somehow incorporated. Including Gaffer, squirming in Nick's arms, mouth again firmly in the lad's grip, one eye on Siren. He'll stay that way until Siren is heavy into scent mode, and out of his field of vision.

'Sebastian, keep your crew at a distance.'

Crew? She is obviously having trouble knowing what to call us.

'I had considered directing Nick and the dog to stay behind on the beach, but should the suspect make an attempt to escape, he could end up here, which might prove more dangerous.'

The dog has a name. Make no wonder he's acting impatient. I am, too. I think we're wasting valuable time.

'Under no circumstances should you people be anywhere but behind us, following my directions.'

Now it's *you people?*

'Understood?' she adds.

'Absolutely,' says Nick, who's just relieved to be joining in.

'Now then, Jude, it's my understanding there's a footpath that leads to an old cemetery. There's the ruins of a church. And several house foundations. I'm assuming there are no structures as such that anyone could inhabit.'

'Correct.'

'Good, that means he likely brought a tent. Which doesn't offer him a protected sightline.'

For *you people* this translates to: trying to fend off cops from inside a tent would be plain stupid.

'This doesn't mean,' says the inspector, 'that he won't pose a danger. Exercise extreme caution at all times.'

I could shake my head at this point. What's Ig going to do—throw hand grenades from behind stunted juniper? The man might have intentionally poisoned someone, but he's not an idiot.

'Jude, feel free to tell us where you think he might have headed, given he needed to pitch a tent. But stay back, allow Siren to take the lead after he picks up the scent.'

A reasonable game plan I'm sure. If I'm skeptical I don't show it.

The church ruins prove a bust. Nothing doing in the cemetery. Obviously Ig was in too much of a hurry to sightsee.

Then, just as Jude predicted from the beginning, Siren's nose locks onto the scent along the footpath that leads to the west side of the island. 'Black Duck Cove,' Jude calls ahead to an overly satisfied and excited Corporal Watten. 'People lived there at one time. Nothing left now.'

Except the newly tented resident whom the lead squad would seem to be anticipating. Prematurely, to my mind. Anyone trying to escape attention is not about to position himself near the open shoreline of an abandoned community, in full view of anyone who might show up.

The squad and the subsidiary unit trailing it eventually break over a grassy hill with the inlet of Black Duck Cove in the distance below. Beyond it are the open waters of Smith Sound. A charming and inviting sight, but even Nick has no interest in whipping out a phone for a selfie.

No deviation from the task at hand, as Siren reminds us. He is tugging his master in the direction of the shoreline.

'You folks, stay here. We need to scout the area. Wait for the all-clear from me before joining us.'

Yes we *folks* are prepared to do just that. If no one else does, Gaffer appreciates the respite. He's not used to trailing a hard-boiled sniffer dog, who herself is leaving a powerful scent.

Nick joins his pal on the grass, saying nothing. I detect a retreat into himself. 'How ya doin'? Okay?'

'Okay.'

'You're worried about what's going on with Ig.'

'Would the cop really use that rifle?'

Fitting what's happening into some context is tough stuff. Framing his relationship with Ig against what he knows of the outside world. Police. Politics. Riots. All impossible to tune out these days.

He knows cops have an image problem. He's had to square that with his daily dose of living with Olsen. And my cynicism likely doesn't help any.

'The rifle's a precaution.'

He's struggling to come back with something more. That makes two of us. Some things are better left unsaid.

'A cop's got a split second to make up his mind,' injects Jude, who neither of us realized has been paying any attention. 'Not good.'

No help for sure. But there it is, another opinion, forcing the kid to weigh all the angles, fighting to figure out one that works for him. One that, I pray like hell, doesn't freak him out.

'Not an easy job,' Jude says. 'Man, I wouldn't want it.'

'It takes a certain type.' To which I immediately add, 'Not thinking of Fred, Nick. Thinking of myself. I wouldn't make much of a cop.'

'I've run into plenty over the years,' Jude says. 'You know Mounties, they get posted some place, and the next thing you hear they're gone again, and someone else shows up. Most of them are not half bad. You run into a few who think they're king shit, but most are, you know, half-decent.'

Nick hints at a smile. *King shit* two days in a row. Not such a relic after all.

It's not much longer when we get the all-clear, come-on-down arm wave from Inspector Bowmore. I suspect they haven't found much. No Ig, but a possible sign of him.

Make that an empty plastic Royal Reserve flask, of recent age, which appears to have washed ashore. And, found near the remnants of a fire, a broken bottle of barbecue sauce.

'Someone was careless,' I offer, in an attempt to give it more significance than it likely deserves.

'Or drunk,' says Jude. That would have been my second guess.

Nick bends over the bottle in an attempt to reassemble the broken pieces mentally. He picks up one piece for a closer look. 'Looks like an "I".' Then another piece. 'And "s . . . l . . . a . . . n . . . d". I – sland. Underneath it—"sauceco". I say it rhymes with Costco.'

'Island Sauce Company,' says Jude, earning him even more respect. Some people have the gift.

Nick fills in more. 'Cape. Smokey. BBQ.'

'Never heard of it,' says Jude. 'And I've tried them all, at least what you can get in the Clarenville Co-op.'

Obviously, if the bottle belonged to Ig, he had a varied taste in grocery stores. I shake my head. I think we're barking up a very deficient tree. Surely to God the RCMP can do better than this.

I hate to be the one to say it, but Black Duck Cove has all the makings of a dead end. On both sides the shoreline terminates with the saltwater splashing against a wall of rock crowned with a thick expanse of trees. Impenetrable for any sane hiking man.

Inspector Bowmore turns to Jude. Good to see. Finally, local knowledge outweighing police ego. 'What do you think?' she asks.

In fact Jude has been thinking a lot. 'The man would have two choices. North, which is basically straight shoreline, thickly wooded, no place to pitch a tent, besides which it would be a hell of a foolish thing to do. Or south, over this ridge. Some woods to get through but mostly barrens, bringing him into Broad Cove. And if there's nothing doing there, at least we'll have open elevation to give us a clear view of everything past that.'

There now, decision made.

We head off together in the direction of Broad Cove. Our unit has been blessed with an invitation to join the big boys up ahead. Not quite equals, but a step in the right direction.

Yet, not surprisingly, and despite the renewed quest to get their man, the RCMP lot has something else bugging them. Why isn't the intrepid Siren picking up a scent?

Gaffer, for one, has no sympathy for the super-sniffer, albeit from the safety of my arms. The uneven terrain has proven a bit exhausting for the lad, plus barking at an unfocused Siren would have proven too much to resist.

The question on everyone's mind is not finding an answer. Clearly, nobody is about to suggest that Siren might not be up to the challenge, resulting in dog and master having to spend the remainder of the trek with their respective tails between their legs. No, better that fellow officer Simmons offers something, anything that could serve as an explanation. 'Inclement weather?'

Really, Sergeant Simmons. Overnight rain selectively soaking up the scent.

Nobody bothers to comment further. In fact there's very little said for the twenty minutes it takes to get to Broad Cove. To no one's surprise, it's as empty of human habitation as the cove we left.

Only Siren shows any measure of excitement. 'He's picked up something,' declares Corporal Watten, elated at the prospect that the canine might have redeemed herself.

The something is an empty beer can, lying among the rocks, just up from the shoreline. Whether, in fact, it has a redemptive scent is open to question. Siren appears to be wandering away from it.

Litter, whichever way you look at it. More litter. I have a visceral reaction to litter, the bane of a tour guide's existence. This discarded can proves even more baneful than most.

'Big Spruce Brewing,' Olsen reads. 'Oatmeal Stout.' Here, he hesitates.

'Anything else?' Ailsa prompts.

'Cereal Killer,' he reads.

Collective recoil.

'C-e-r-e-a-l,' he clarifies.

'Where's it made?'

Olsen turns the can and reads the fine print. 'Baddeck, Nova Scotia.'

There you go. I look over at Jude. Is he thinking what I'm thinking?

'The bugger of an owner, whoever he is, wouldn't even support the local economy by buying our beer,' Jude declares. 'Open up the Atlantic Bubble and here they come, coolers full of their own stuff, ready to litter the place with the empty cans.'

The Bubble can be a powder keg. No question about it. The RCMP foursome resist entering the fray, ingrained as they are to remaining politically neutral. Yet it's incumbent on Inspector Bowmore to address the subject of the alien can. 'It's unlikely that it came from the suspect. May well have been thrown from a passing boat and washed up on the rocks.'

'Thrown overboard by some thoughtless yahoo. Makes you wonder.' Jude needs a final two cents' worth.

As the inspector sees it, there's no point in lingering over another dead end. She's ready to move on. Which, by the look of the terrain ahead, will be no easy feat.

Jude's local knowledge—indispensable yet again. At the tentative encouragement of Inspector Bowmore, he takes the lead. Tentative, to ward off the notion that the RCMP might not have a clue what to do next.

Jude, riding high on his beer can rant, is gung-ho.

He quickly embraces his new position, setting a pace that challenges the physical dexterity of Siren and her team. To say nothing of Gaffer's team, the older member of which struggles to keep them all in sight. Damn it all, Jude, you don't have to work so hard at dispelling the stereotype of the wharf-bound fisherman with a cigarette hanging from his lip. I believe you, you're bloody fit!

It doesn't help any that I stumble and smack myself in the face with a dead tree branch. Out of breath and pissed, I'm not ready for Nick running back with Gaffer and urging me on in a loud whisper, 'Dad, hurry up, you're not going to believe this!'

Believe what? That we've reached another dead end? That Jude has his mind set on another damn obstacle course?

No, what I don't believe is all five of them plus two dogs no longer upright, but flat on their guts, spread across lichen-covered rock that overlooks the shoreline below and off from it an island no more than fifty metres at its widest point and on which is pitched a bright orange tent, with an equally bright yellow, inflatable kayak hauled up next to it. That's what I don't believe.

Olsen motions me to the ground. He's playing ad hoc bodyguard to Nick, who's within arm's length of him. I sink down, pitching tight to Nick's other side, Gaffer wedged in rigid suspense between us.

From that angle I can see the scope and barrel of the rifle Simmons has been toting this whole trek, projected ahead of us and aimed at the tent. Is that even bloody necessary?

It's paired with the high-powered binoculars that Ailsa is holding to her eyes. She has a brief few words with Jude to the right of her, before the row of officers retreat into themselves, submerging into deep, hushed conversation, a bloody veritable cone of silence covering them.

Ailsa finally decides to break it, reluctantly I conclude.

Her mental sweat is showing. Crest of a cliff, breeze off the saltwater hitting her square in the face, suspect ensconced in some space-age fabric on a treeless square of island. Obviously she's not had to deal with a situation quite like this before. Clearly not covered in RCMP training exercises.

Despite that, a brave face. 'We need to get closer to the suspect. There's a short stretch of shoreline directly below us and across from the island. And there appears to be a route we can take to get to it.'

Jude confirms the plan. 'A little rough in places, but we're good to go.'

'In the meantime,' the inspector adds, 'Sergeant Simmons will remain here and give us cover.'

Olsen jumps in. 'Nick, for safety reasons, you and Gaffer are to stay behind as well. And Sebastian, since you know this man, we're asking you to join us, given that your relationship could prove an asset.'

Oh, it can prove an asset all right. No worries there, Mr. Second-in-Command.

But he's not done yet. 'You're unarmed, so prepare to pull back out of sight, should the situation warrant it.'

I ignore the hired hand and go straight to the boss. 'Ig is not your crazed criminal, Inspector Bowmore. I'd appreciate some slack.'

It doesn't play well. She ignores it.

Rather, she sets the RCMP plan in motion. Nick (and Gaffer for that matter) is none too pleased to be left behind, but they have no choice in the matter. Actually, I agree with Olsen on that one. Safer, he's right. And one less thing for me to worry about. Nick holds up a disgruntled hand in response to my thumbs-up. I disappear from sight, tailgating those ahead while I can.

The descent, for the vertically challenged like myself, is emphatically steep. Jake does his best to forge a diagonal route, but with limited success. Siren and his handler in particular have met their match. It would seem the police dog school in Alberta did little to prepare the sniffer for a precipitous descent through dense and gnarled undergrowth in Newfoundland. At least she can dispense with sniffing and set her focus on reaching a destination.

You've got to give Ig credit for his attempt to shake off any pursuers with the kayak. No doubt he wouldn't be expecting pursuit by such a tenacious lot. One that eventually emerges near the shoreline relatively unscathed, shielded behind a clump of tuckamore, the stunted evergreen more than adequate cover for five adults and a canine.

If this all seems surreal, that's because it is. All this effort in pursuit of a guy stuck on a scrap of an island with absolutely zero chance of escape. The inflatable kayak is sure as hell not going to do it. And, what the fuck, like he's about to come charging out of that tent and fend off four armed cops.

'Really, folks, let's get serious here. Call off the calvary.'

To say it's not appreciated by the Royal Canadian Mounted Police is clearly an understatement. Cops set themselves in a definite frame of mind and come hell or high water they're going to stick with it. In a crisis, flexibility is not their strong suit. What they don't get is that it's not a crisis. It's Ig in a bloody tent.

'Sebastian, you'll have to remain here. We'll call on you when we need you.'

Put me in my place, why don't you, Inspector Bowmore. I'm well aware you're in police professional mode, but the least you can do, crouched behind tuckamore, is be civil.

Nevertheless, I come to attention and follow orders. I have Jude to share in the fucking chagrin.

The three cops advance to the shore, handguns drawn, rifle above them primed and ready. The stage is set, the drama begins.

'Mr. Payne!' Inspector Bowmore calls across the thirty metres of water to the island. 'This is the RCMP. You are under arrest. Come out with your hands in the air. We are armed and prepared to shoot.'

Seriously cliché.

There is dead silence. Zero indication of movement inside the tent. Ears fine-tuned for the sound of unzipping. Nothing.

'Mr. Payne. I repeat, you are under arrest. Cooperate and nothing will happen to you. I repeat, come out with your hands in the air.'

Except for the indifferent lap of waves against the shores, nothing.

The cops glance at each other. Attempting to come to terms with what their next move might be.

'Mr. Payne . . .'

This time followed by a bark.

A distinctive bark. An 'arf' with an 'h' bark. Gaffer's.

'Harf, harf, harf, harf . . . !' And even more intense. 'Harf, harf, harf, harf . . . !'

Good God, Nick knows better than to allow that to happen. The RCMP rears up.

Abruptly, a gunshot overhead!

Holy fuck!

Nothing.

Bark, for fuck's sake, Gaffer, bark!

I take off, tearing my way back up the incline, driving a way through with all that's in me. The first time I stumble and smack my head against a tree, Jude drags me to my feet and forces me to follow him. I chase after him blindly, a terrified father praying desperately that Nick is all right. Gaffer, too. Jesus.

We get near the top, break into the open, and there's Nick, several metres away, sitting on the ground, clutching a quivering Gaffer with one hand, holding the dog's jaws shut with the other.

Thank God. Thank God. I'm bent forward, my hands gripping my thighs for support. Massive relief between laboured breaths.

Upright now, about to stride in Nick's direction, I catch sight of Sergeant Simmons out of the corner of my eye. Sweet fuck. Gagged and roped to a runt of a tree.

Jude taps me on the shoulder. I look behind and bolt even further upright.

A rifle is pointed straight at me. Behind it a man in full camouflage. A fucker looking like a moose hunter. Except for his rifle, the RCMP standard issue Colt C8.

'How's it goin', Sebastian?'

What the fucking hell?

'Take a closer look.' He lowers the rifle enough that I get a view of his face.

Jesus Christ. Alistair McDuff.

On the fucking *Rock(s)* Alistair McDuff.

He lowers the rifle further and lets it hang by his side. 'Surprised?'

So surprised I'm fucking struck dumb.

A second camouflaged fellow walks into view from behind him.

The Ig Payne we have all been looking for. 'Sorry about this, Sebastian. Your boy is fine. He's not in any danger.'

'Christ, Ig,' snaps McDuff. 'Fuck off with the charity.'

'What's this shit, Ig?'

'Al Duffett.' That's all he says.

Al Duffett. The best friend Al Duffett, from high school? Al Duffett, now Alistair fucking McDuff?

How did they get here? There's no time to process this.

'You're both screwed! There's more of us, more cops with guns. You haven't got a hope in hell of getting away.'

'Which reminds me,' says Duffett, pointing his weapon in the direction of the woods from where we just emerged. He rapid fires a round of bullets. 'Just so they get the message.'

It shuts me up for a few seconds. Not Jude. 'So, man, you make it back to your boat. You get away. To where, before you run out of gas?'

'You'd like to know, wouldn't you?'

My eyes bore into Ig's. 'Your truck is impounded. You know that.'

'Of course it's impounded!' yells Duffett. 'You think we're bloody stupid?'

'Where did you park your other vehicle?' says Jake.

That hadn't yet registered with me.

'You go ashore,' says Jake, a whole lot calmer than I am, 'and wherever it is the cops will track you down, no matter how long it takes.'

'I told him that,' says Ig.

'Shut up!'

'It was him, not me. I didn't poison the guy.'

'Shut the fuck up!'

'I didn't.'

'You asshole Iggy, you sure as hell went along with it. You sure as hell had a hand on Aub when he went in that water.'

'So did you! He didn't drown because of that. He was drunk. We both figured he'd get back up. We were gone before he drowned.'

Who's he trying to convince? Me?

'And Randy. I dropped in enough to get him sick, not kill him.'

Duffett pivots toward him, like it's the first he's heard of it. 'You scum. You bloody scum.' He starts to raise the rifle. 'See this gun. One more is not going to make any fucking difference.'

Ig is obviously shit-baked. 'Al, man, put that down.'

'You screwed up.'

'You got it wrong.'

'We had it planned, and you screwed it up, Iggy. You want me to put a bullet in your friend here? That should even things up. Let's see where your loyalty runs then.'

'We can still do it,' Ig says lamely. 'We can still get away.'

'You want to beg a little louder. How about you put more guts into it.'

'We been through shit together.'

'Apparently not enough. I'm thinking we're due some more.'

He raises the rifle higher.

'Drop it!' Booming from the woods behind him.

'Drop the rifle!'

Bowmore and Olsen. They've emerged from the woods, on different parts of the clearing, handguns straight out in front of them.

'I said, drop it!'

'Now!'

For a second the guy's looking like he's caught in a game. Play it right, and there's escape to be had. Outsmart them because you got the bigger gun. For that second he's the misfit who thinks he can trounce them all.

'I didn't drown the guy. It wasn't me.'

He pulls the trigger, shoots into the air.

The bullets strike his chest in the same split second. He slumps, pitches onto the bare rock. There's a couple of seconds when no one moves. He's undoubtedly dead.

The shock is profound. Was it a madman they just killed?

Silence cuts the air, the aftershock dulling slowly.

Ig stands over him, hands above his head. A pitiful fugitive.

What else will he turn out to be?

A murderer? That's a question the law will weigh.

My concern is not Ig. It's my son. All this time Nick has been sitting on the ground, some distance behind us, holding Gaffer even tighter. He's seen it all.

'I'm okay,' he says, before I have chance to ask.

I help him to his feet. He sets Gaffer down. The dog barks. I cherish the bark. A bark giving relief to all three of us.

'You're sure you're okay?'

'We keep getting in these situations,' Nick says, with the barest hint of a false smile. A failed attempt at lightening the strain.

Olsen wanders over to check on him. He puts a hand on his shoulder.

'I'm sorry I left you here. I wasn't thinking clearly.'

I'm open to sharing the guilt. 'Nobody would have predicted that.'

It's as far as either of us is willing to take it.

'You guys go on back,' Olsen says. 'We'll handle this.'

He turns in the direction he needs to be, having a word with Jude on the way. Siren and Corporal Watten emerge from the woods. The corporal holds back the confused sniffer from pitching into Ig.

Ailsa is looking in our direction as she works at releasing Sergeant Simmons. I hold up a hand to her. Anything else is best left for now. I just want Nick and Gaffer out of here.

Jude makes a move and we're gone, back the way we came.

Eventually we reach the boat. It's a silent ride back to Lower Lance Cove.

I owe Jude something more than the additional money he refuses to take.

'Listen, man, you're all safe. I'm good. You fellows come by some time.' He shakes our hands and rubs Gaffer's head.

'You like Scotch?'

'Try me.'

'Deal, Jude.'

We're gone then. Back to Trinity.

SCENE 2

WITH ONE STOP along the way.

It takes a new, more calculated approach, but I manage an N95 meeting with Randy. It involves seeing a different side to an overworked Dr. Woodruff, one that responds well to fawning.

Randy looks half-decent, at least what I can see of him behind the mask. Not bad for someone getting over a bout with cyanide. He's as eager to see me as I am to see him. He's desperate to know what transpired following the visit he had from the inspectors.

I give him a modified version of the past few hours. Not good to be adding to his stress level, or mine for that matter. Still, it's enough to sharpen his opinion of what happened to him.

'No matter what way you look at it, Ig played the cunt.'

You could say that. If you're Randy. I'm not fond of the word myself, but then again I wasn't lying unconscious, on the way to getting my stomach pumped after drinking Ig's can of Stella Artois.

I need to know the reason behind the tainted beer.

'That morning when I got up I was crawling around the

floor in the living room, looking for some money I thought must have fallen out of my pocket when I was lying on the couch the night before. I came across this yearbook under the couch. I had a look and saw Ig's picture so I figured it must have belonged to him, and had somehow ended up there before he rented the house. So I called over to his place and told him about it.

'While I was waiting for him to show up, I ate breakfast and looked through it some more. The next thing I know I'm looking at a picture of Aubrey Mercer, his name underlined. Even with the long hair he looked so much like Lyle. Same surname so I figured it had to be the cousin who drowned. Suddenly it dawned on me that the yearbook belonged to Lyle. That it wasn't Ig's at all. That's when I texted you.

'Ig eventually showed up, with two beer in his jacket pocket, all thankful I found his missing yearbook. He wanted to talk about it. He even pointed out Aubrey, like he'd been a buddy of his. I know now he was fishing for some indication that I knew who it was.

'That's when I blew it. I said, stupid-like, "I noticed that guy, he looks a lot like Lyle. Was that the cousin who drowned?" Duh!'

Of course, at the time, Randy had no idea Ig had any connection to the drowning. Neither did he know that Ig realized it was only a matter of time before Randy found out from me there was a connection. So better shut Randy up before that happens and get rid of the yearbook before I can lay my eyes on it.

Randy has a deeper question. 'Why do you think he only did half the job on me?'

'My guess is as soon as he got off the phone with you that morning, he called Al Duffett to tell him. Al blew up and said Ig had to get rid of you. Right away, no second thoughts.

Except Ig had second thoughts. He couldn't go through with it, not to the point of killing you at least. Only enough to convince Al he did.'

'Really. Fuck.'

'He figured he could never be charged with murder up to this point. As far as he was concerned Aubrey's drowning was an accident. And Al was the one who had poisoned Lyle. So it was either do the job on you or use only enough of the cyanide that there was a good chance you'd recover. Ig was out to save his own skin somehow.'

'And yours maybe,' says Randy.

To be honest, the thought crossed my mind.

'You had to be next on the list. And it sounds to me this guy Al had a list. He was in so far over his head, or off his head, whatever, that he didn't give a shit who else he killed. Maybe it was Ig's way of saving you.'

Good to think that way, that Ig had it in him. Good for Nick, if nothing else.

It'll take time to sort it out.

Our talk makes Randy all the more anxious to get out of the hospital. He's already decided he wants nothing more to do with Trouty. I agree to pack up his belongings and take them with me. After he's discharged he'll make his way to St. John's and Jess.

As for Jess, she's pretty stressed out still, according to Randy. So much so that once she was sure he was on the mend, she just wanted to get away from it all, get it behind her. Their Grenfell courses are online this fall because of COVID, so no need to be in Corner Brook. They'll rent a place together in St. John's and do them remotely.

'When you come by to pick up your stuff,' I tell him, 'we'll continue your Scotch tutorial.'

Fist bump to that.

When I reach the parking lot I discover the Mercers from Keels getting out of their pickup. I shouldn't be surprised. They would have known Randy from visiting Lyle in Trouty. They heard what happened.

'He's all right, is he?'

'He's good. Another couple of days in the hospital.' Which has to be bittersweet considering what happened to their son.

'Do you think the two incidents are related, Mr. Synard?'

It's better they don't know and I certainly won't be the one to tell them. 'It's possible. The police have it under investigation.'

'The rumour is they're looking for Ig Payne,' says Vickie. 'Someone posted it on one of my chat rooms.'

Chat rooms? And we think outports aren't tuned to technology.

'I'm not sure.'

'No surprise to us,' Stan adds. 'He's a strange one. The first time I met him I asked him if he happened to know a fellow by the name of Aubrey Mercer and he said he never heard of him. Which I figured had to be a lie because he just finished telling me he grew up in Trinity.'

'Put two and two together,' says Vickie. 'Guilty as sin.'

They're desperate to find someone accountable for what happened to their son. Time is the great healer, it's said. We can all reflect on that at some level. But in this case I'm doubtful if time will complete the task. I look at them as they walk slowly, side by side towards the hospital entrance. In all that's happened over the past few weeks they're the people who have lost the most. I can't think their hearts will ever truly mend.

We need to wrap things up with Donna.

For the time being at least. We take to the benches on the wharf outside the theatre for a final chat before heading back home in the morning.

'Caught the acting bug, have you?' she says to Nick.

He concedes as much with his smile and shrug combination.

'I did you some good then. And you know actors— strapped for cash for the rest of their lives. Your old man will be forever grateful.'

Laughter between them at my expense. I'll take that. I'll take Nick acting like he wasn't frightened out of his mind a few hours ago.

'Anytime you need my advice, you call me.'

Right. Lamb to the slaughter.

Nick gives her an impish thumbs-up as he heads off with Gaffer.

'He's a terrific kid,' she says. 'You're doing a great job.'

When it comes down to it, Donna always finds the right thing to say.

She's in no way prepared for what I'm about to tell her. But she's due a solid version of the story, without the details that the RCMP wouldn't want to be public knowledge at this point. Details that could then be traced back to me. Not good.

As it is, I swear her to secrecy.

Her reaction can be summed up in a few well-chosen words. 'Jesus Christ,' she says under her breath, as if it tempers the blasphemy. 'What the fuck got into them?' Donna always was good at getting to the crux of the matter.

'It all goes back to that one night forty years ago. Teenage horseplay that went wrong. Because of it, three people ended up dead.'

'You really think it was unintentional?'

'I do. Ig Payne would never have killed Aubrey Mercer, as much as he detested the guy. Or Al Duffett for that matter, who had even less reason to do away with him. It happened and they spent their lives hoping it would be forgotten. Ig was so sure it was that he came back home. And then Lyle showed up. They had all those years of coming to terms with the fact that someone might figure out what really happened, and when someone did, they got desperate.'

'Poison him rather than let it play out and count on nothing ever being proven?'

'You get older, you're less willing to take the chance. Maybe you're not thinking straight. From what I saw of him, Al didn't have a lot going for him in the straight-thinking department.'

'You figure without him Lyle would still be alive?'

'We'll never know for sure. Ig Payne is a complicated man. He played a part that I don't think he believed in. You know yourself, if an actor doesn't buy into a role, it never works.'

'By God, Sebastian, I taught you something when I hired you.'

It works to relieve the tension.

'Take it from me,' she says, 'there's more than two sides to every story.'

She doesn't need any encouragement.

'There's a few things I've learned from a lifetime in theatre,' she says. 'Some of them you wouldn't want to know.' She chuckles. 'But one is—you put a character on stage and sure as hell he's not entirely what he seems. Theatre is all about digging into that enigma.'

'*One man in his time plays many parts.*'

'You know your Shakespeare.'

'I have my untold self.'

'Like our Mr. Payne.'

I tell her about the accident, the loss of his son. It quiets the conversation. Adds more to the enigma.

'It never stopped playing on his mind, that's for sure,' she says.

There's little point in hashing it out any more. It feels like Donna would give me all the time in the world, but we'd still be no closer to any answers. It's time we moved on, shifted directions.

'It clears the air as far as Rising Tide is concerned.'

'Now all I have to worry about is a pandemic.'

'There's promising news on the vaccine front,' I point out.

'Bring on your vaccinated masses! We need an audience.'

I'll miss her. I'll miss the laughs, the willingness to speak her mind, the generosity, the energy.

But Nick and I and Gaffer have to get back to St. John's. School is starting up again and the boy needs to settle into his regular routine.

As for him being able to leave all that's happened behind, that remains to be seen. By keeping him focused on packing up, tidying the house, sitting down to the frozen pizza we just pulled out of the oven—for the moment at least he appears to be back in the real world.

Not so fast. He barely touches the pizza. Admittedly it's a quick fix, nothing like what we've been known to cook from scratch, but still, he must be hungry. Gaffer looks up at him, more than willing to down his portion.

'I know, it's been a rough day.' Downplaying is maybe the best option at this point.

Nick responds, blatantly serious. 'I never thought I'd ever see anyone shot and killed. What's on their minds when they pull the trigger?'

Best option or not, it didn't take. 'In this case they had no choice. The fellow had a rifle and, given the chance, he would have used it.'

'Still, something went through their minds.'

'Cops are trained to kill, given the circumstance.'

'I don't think I could do it.'

'That's good. There was a time I'd say the same thing.'

'You mean if you'd had a gun . . .'

'To protect someone I love, absolutely.'

He's thinking about it.

'You're wondering what was going through Fred's mind?'

'Maybe.'

'I think I know. You. He had you in his mind.'

That sets him back.

'He wasn't about to take a chance on you getting hurt.'

'But I wasn't in danger. I was out of the picture.'

'Not really. The guy holding the rifle knew right where you were. One quick swing of the gun.'

I regret saying it. It might be true, although I'm thinking it's not likely Duffett was in that headspace. Why say it, then? Why put it out there when Nick already has too much to deal with?

'Fred thinks the world of you.' I can't bring myself to say "love". Which says a lot about me I'm sure. 'He definitely wasn't about to take that chance.'

Nick takes his time. 'Dad, ever think it was you Fred was protecting? Maybe you were next on the guy's list.'

He's catching on. Smarter by the day.

'Now there's a thought.' Might as well smile at it. Can't come up with anything better.

Nick is filling up.

'It's okay, pal. It didn't happen.'

'Fuck,' he blurts out.

I walk to the other side of the table and hug his head into my chest. 'Hey, pal, watch the language,' I choke out, past my own tears.

We're washing up the dishes when a knock comes on the door.

It's Stephanie. My plan was to see her before we left in the morning. She looks terrible. I should have realized it couldn't wait.

'I can't stay long.' We sit in the living room, the three of us and Gaffer, who takes a spot on the couch, curled up near her. Dogs, I swear, can sense when someone needs comforting. Stephanie strokes him as we talk.

The RCMP called her an hour ago. Ig has been detained, awaiting an appearance in court. She's talked to him. It's all been overwhelming, to say the least. A lot of unanswered questions.

Some I do my best to answer. Some it's better she takes to the police. It seems Ig was reluctant to tell her much. I'm left uncertain just how much.

'I had no idea Al Duffett was even near the place,' she says, holding back her emotion. 'You'd have thought someone would have recognized him.'

I assume Ig convinced her Al Duffett was solely responsible for poisoning Lyle. I'm wondering now if Ig realized I was the one leading the tour that brought Al to Trinity.

I tread carefully. 'It was so long ago that Al left. He grew a beard, lost his hair. Wore a mask in public. Maybe he was back in Trinity only long enough to do what he did.'

'Ig must have met up with him.'

'Not necessarily. The police will analyze Ig's cellphone. It could be they just talked. Maybe Ig's first face-to-face contact with him was when Ig picked him up in his boat yesterday.'

'I don't understand. I don't understand. They're saying Ig must have had the poison in the house.' Her thoughts are disjointed. She's jumped to the incident with Randy.

'Then maybe Al did get the poison to him, somehow. Just in case. We'll never know how the guy's brain operated.'

It's better if she's thinking that. Better than her having to deal with the other scenario, that Ig procured it himself.

'Just in case what?'

'That someone else got nosey.' That's one answer. Another

is something I've thought about but am not about to raise with Stephanie. Suicide. Was there ever a point where Ig figured it all might become too much for him to deal with? That he himself was better off dead?

Nick is finding it tough seeing Stephanie so frantic for answers. He's struggling for something to say. The young fellow spent more time with Ig than I did, but I'm thinking now it's a mistake for him to even be in the room.

'Ig told me about Ryan,' he says to her.

For a second I'm confused. Then it dawns on me that Ryan was the son who died in the accident. And that Nick knew about him all along, even his name, which I didn't.

A stark few words. Nick strains to come up with more. He wants her to know about the relationship he had with Ig. That the two of them got to be friends.

He sort of shrugs, but not quite. Awkward reassurance for her.

It brings Stephanie to tears of course. She doesn't find the words either.

She strokes Gaffer a final time and stands up to leave.

'I hope it all turns out for the best,' I say as she's about to go through the door. Cold comfort to a woman clearly in the need of consolation. I am, after all, the one who led the police to her husband, who most likely will be called at some point to testify in court.

She looks at me. 'Good night.'

She turns to Nick and with some hesitancy circles him in her arms. He's caught by surprise, unsure it's the right thing to do, but he brings his arms loosely around her.

It only lasts a second before she turns and goes. As she walks across the road I see there is a car parked in front of her house. I hope it belongs to family or friends. She needs them.

SCENE 3

THE HOUSE ON Military Road feels very distant from the one we left in Trouty. I'm comfortable here. I fit the space I'm in, something I haven't felt all the time I was gone. Gaffer thinks much the same way. We're a reasonably contented pair.

Gaffer will often rest his chin on the corner of the laptop as I write, but this afternoon he has opted for pure, unencumbered sleep. There's the occasional twitch and mutter, the high point of a dream no doubt, but he settles quickly back to the charmed life he's come to know in this, our comfy chair.

As have I. The dram in hand is a new discovery. A sanely priced gem from Islay—Bruichladdich Port Charlotte 10-year-old. Branded as "heavily peated".

Make that "heavenly peated". Occasionally my favoured NLC outlet will knock me back with what it sneaks onto its shelves. Good going, you've hit me with your best shot. Fire away.

Focus, Sebastian. I have to decide what book to pair it with for my whisky blog. As I discover, not a long process. Viet Thanh Nguyen has a new book out. Loved *The Sympathizer*. Not only that, my online foraging for background information reveals the author is a Scotch demon. Loves the peat, the straight, unadulterated dram. Look no farther.

My iPhone suddenly comes alive. Gaffer twitches but has no interest in answering it. It's up to me. I fish the phone out of my pocket. Ah, Olsen. I've been expecting a call, although with no confidence as to when exactly the good inspector might get in touch. The man prefers being unpredictable. It adds to his potency.

'Fred, my man . . .'

If I sound more amiable than usual it's because he has been forced to take some of the heat from Nick's recent brush with danger. Samantha, to put it mildly, was not impressed when the story emerged. Nick's attempt at downplaying it failed miserably, I gather, under incessant probing from his mother. According to Nick, Fred then told all, leaving her torn between berating me and berating the man who shares the expanse of her bed. I got the brunt of it. No surprise there. But as for the other, it made for some quote/unquote (Nick again) "moderate fireworks".

'Nick tells me you're no worse for wear.' I leave it open as to which battlefield I'm referring to, professional or domestic. I enjoy the ambiguity.

'It's never easy.'

It catches me unprepared. He means the pulling of the trigger. The cut of his words, solemn and inconclusive, leave no doubt.

Our island is not prone to gun violence. Up to a couple of decades ago the RNC didn't even carry sidearms. I doubt the officer has put a bullet in a man before, at least not enough to put an end to him. I don't ask.

'Rough stuff.'

That's about the best that men can do. Yet, we're still able to read each other.

'I'm calling to let you know what we found out about the casualty.'

'Good man.'

'Legally he was Alastair McDuff. He changed his name shortly after he moved to Nova Scotia. That would have been in the early 1980s. We talked to his aunt in Trinity. She appears to be the sole relative he has left there. He was back home a couple of times, but the last was more than twenty years ago, to attend his parents' funerals.'

His body has been sent to Cape Breton for burial, although there was trouble finding anyone willing to take on the responsibility. Eventually Cape Breton police were able to track down an estranged daughter.

'No other family?'

'A granddaughter.'

He's hesitating. God, I'm thinking, here it comes. I can't hold my breath any longer. 'Her name wouldn't happen to be Jess?'

He keeps me waiting. 'As it turns out . . . I'm sorry to have to tell you . . . no.'

The big frigger. Who's now chuckling to himself no doubt. 'Your Jess is in the clear.'

'Good.' I don't give him the satisfaction of anything more.

'Very good, actually. We interviewed her, as you know. Turned out to be a lovely girl. Her father lives in New Brunswick. He came to see her in July. He's a judge, as a matter of fact.'

Enough said. As tempting as it is, I don't try to score on Olsen's miscalculation.

'What's happening with Ig?'

'Out on bail. Under house arrest, pending further investigation.'

He sticks to the facts. I know there's no point in trying to dig deeper, especially considering that for this investigation he's only one cog in the police wheel. Still, he called. He didn't have to.

Although there's another reason he called, something other than to keep me clued in on the case. He wants to talk about Nick. And is not sure how to go about it. The usually cut-and-dried cop struggles to get to the point.

When he finally does, he's worked himself into a sweat. 'Listen, Sebastian, I don't want to get personal about all this but Nick's going through something.'

Teenagers are always going through something. Plus, he's just started his first year of high school. Plus, he's having one heck of a growth spurt. 'What exactly?'

'His mother worries about him.'

Dodging the question, for no good reason as far as I can tell. 'Why doesn't she talk to me herself?'

'I'm trying to convince her she should.'

Which means he's going behind her back to approach me. That, or she's asked him to do the dirty work for her. Neither of which sit well with me.

'Fred, I hate to say it, but this shit is going nowhere.'

'She's wondering if he might be gay.'

Wondering? What the frig is Samantha going on about?

He's expecting me to be surprised. I'm not. 'Nick and I have already had this discussion. Like a year ago. We dealt with it. If it turns out he is, he is.'

His sweat intensifies. 'Not going there,' he says. 'Not my place.'

'Listen, you tell Samantha to cut the crap and call me. You're not his father, I am.'

'I more than realize that. I'm not liking this any more than you are. She's saying any talk with Nick is better coming from a man. She thinks he's not going to open up to his mother.'

'Bullshit.'

'Okay, okay.'

He wants off the phone. It's as plain as his audible breath.

'Good luck.' Odd fucking thing to say I know. I had to end it somehow. I jab the end icon before he sweats some more.

Now I'm thinking Samantha asked Olsen to have "the talk" and he wants out of it. And so he bloody well should.

I try to calm down. If I give Samantha the benefit of the doubt (not so frigging easy in this case) then I should admit she's under a shitload of stress at the moment, with schools reopening for in-person classes after being locked down since last March. The job of school principal exhausted her at the best of times; now she has all the COVID restrictions coming at her. Stress enough to mismanage something to do with her son? No.

Nick goes to a different high school, thankfully. He's at Holy Heart, up the street from the junior high he just left. Actual full name: Holy Heart of Mary. Sounding very Catholic, which it was until the education system in Newfoundland switched from religion-based to public. They kept the name. (Which, I might add, is one mouthful up from a couple of elementary schools: Mary, Queen of Peace and Mary, Queen of the World.) The Blessed Virgin did well by us in Newfoundland. Nevertheless, by all reports Holy Heart is a very good school.

The kid is due any minute. Except I can't be calling him kid anymore. I swear he's grown an inch in the last month. Must be all that fresh air. He started late, but he's sure as heck hitting his stride now. Maybe that's all part of it. Maybe the hormone surge is driving Samantha over the edge.

Gaffer is on all four paws and at the door before Nick even gets to it. I tell Nick his adolescent odour precedes him. It's one of our running jokes.

In he comes, six-foot in the making. Gaffer is not used to

climbing so high.

'Hey, Nick, what's up? Way up.'

But it's not Nick I see first. It's the friend who he's jostled in ahead of him. Both boys with their masks hanging below their chins, no doubt a lightning manoeuvre the second they broke free of school.

'Dad, this is Kofi. Kofi, say hello to my dad.'

'Hello, sir.'

Shy politeness. Not the friend Tyler I've been used to. And with a more interesting background, obviously.

'Come in, Kofi. Have a seat. Any relation to Kofi Annan?'

'Same country but no, sir.' What country I don't quite remember.

When Nick takes to the sofa, Gaffer jumps up and goes straight for Kofi, overwhelming him with his standard face-licking antics.

'Down, Gaffer, down,' Nick tells him, which, as usual, Gaffer ignores, until Nick physically makes him sit between him and his friend.

'So Kofi, your first year at Holy Heart?'

'Yes, sir.'

'He transferred in from St. Paul's.'

Which is not the junior high that Nick went to. Which means they only met recently. I like this. I like the fact Nick is making new friends. I like the fact he's expanded beyond his old peer group. Maybe he's outgrown Tyler. I won't be disappointed if he has.

'Kofi and I signed up for Performing Arts.'

Am I surprised? (I thank you, Donna. At least at this point.)

'Me for acting. Kofi's doing tech.'

'Way to go, guys.'

'And guess what—Kofi likes to cook.'

'I help out my mother sometimes.'

'His parents have a spot at the Farmer's Market, on week-ends.'

'Kumasi Kitchen.'

'We know it, right Nick? We've had the jollof rice.'

'My specialty,' says Kofi.

This is all doing my heart good. Up to this point I've been thinking—teenager starting off in a new school, trying to fit in, bound to be problems. And now I'm thinking—what's all this crap you're going on with, Samantha. The boy's found a friend who likes to cook. A recipe for questioning sexual orientation? Give me a break.

'Tell you what, Kofi, you come by sometime and teach us how to make jollof rice and we'll teach you how to make . . . I dunno . . .'

'Sex-in-a-pan,' says Nick, and breaks out laughing. 'I told Kofi about sex-in-a-pan. He thought it was revolting.'

He's purposely embarrassing the poor guy. Although it's not long before Kofi is also cracking up.

No point in denying the fact that after Nick and I had "the talk", deficient as it was, I don't look at his relationships with his friends in the same way. And that includes wondering whether they do more than laugh about sex. I can't help it. Out of touch with the realities of teenage life, generational gap, whatever. I am what I am, and that would be fifty-something.

Drive all that out of the picture for the time being, and get back to liking the fact they are friends. That Nick has redirected his life, expanded his world, and taken up acting. Sounds like he won't have time to be bored. Less screen time, more real time.

This is good.

If I appear somewhat on edge, it is for a very good reason. Ailsa (not to be confused with Inspector Bowmore) has invited me to dinner, at her apartment. We're still within our expanded bubbles, so no masking required. Our respective facial reactions displayed to the wider world—should be interesting.

The invitation was by email, which, as I see it, I can interpret in one of two ways. Either Ailsa is uncertain how the evening will unfold and for now prefers to keep the neutral tone of a written communication. Or she is about to terminate any scrap of personal relationship with one final positive gesture (i.e., a home-cooked meal), but doesn't want to risk giving away her intention in a phone call.

Neither of them positive. To be honest, I feel like I'm heading to a requiem for a relationship. I bring along flowers, in keeping with the expectation. And a bottle of wine, should it prove wrong.

I ring the doorbell with an open mind. Ailsa answers it with a broad smile. The hit-or-miss evening begins. I slip the wine onto the kitchen counter while she slips the flowers into some water. 'This is very sweet of you. I love alstroemeria.'

Sounds good. Not that I had any hope of calling them by name. First I thought roses, but then thought, no, too strong a statement. Better a bouquet of neutral whatever. Which now (load off my mind) has turned out to be the perfect choice.

'And I hope you like Prosecco.' Again, calculated neutrality. Who doesn't like Prosecco?

'Why don't we give it a go?'

Give it a go? Surprising choice of words. Give it a go? Absolutely. Does the phrase have potential for setting the tone for the evening? I don't build up hope.

I was expecting a little less congeniality, a little more chill. As we take to the living room to partake of olives, brie, and charcuterie, I lean slightly towards cautious optimism. Even more so since she shows, at this stage at least, no inclination to talk business.

I'm all for that. Keep the investigation at a distance. Allow room for the more immediate matters of everyday life. 'Good news on the vaccine front.'

'Terrific news.'

'A light at the end of the tunnel.'

'I can't wait. Really looking forward to making a trip to Ontario.'

That would be very far down on my to-do list, but, of course, she has family there.

'Hopefully before long.'

The thrust of initial conversation fades to monotone, which continues past the shrimp curry and mango salad. The pitch barely rises during the intake of the intense flourless chocolate cake topped with rum-flavoured whipped cream. By the time the lattes show up we've pretty well exhausted the immediate and slipped into the mundane. 'Beautiful September so far. Temperatures still double-digit.'

Only the Laphroaig 18, awaiting us on our reentry into the living room, boosts the conversation current, sending it veering in a new direction. Laphroaig has a tendency to do that.

As does the fact that I've taken a seat next to her on the sofa, without first considering there was any need to ask.

If she does mind she doesn't show it. What she does do is set her whisky glass on the coffee table in front of us.

'There's something I need to tell you.'

Okay. I agree. It has to come to this. There's no escaping it.

'Give it a go.' The line falls away, unnoticed.

'If there was any chance of it working out, I'd be willing to try. But let's be realistic. Our lives conflict on too many levels.'

She is a take-charge kind of woman. Got to admire that. Got to admire the urge to get to the root of the problem.

'You mean don't let any attraction we have for each other get in the way.'

I wouldn't say she's ready for that. She looks away, looks straight ahead at nothing. Calculating what her response should be, stressed to get it right.

To me, there is no right, as such. I put my own glass on the table. I quietly place my hand on hers.

It takes a moment, but she responds. 'Shit.'

I like the ambiguity. I find that particular four-letter word so variable in its meaning. If I interpret her intonation correctly, she's saying "shit, where do we go from here?"

It seems to me there comes a time in a relationship when actions speak louder than words. I look at her until she finally turns her head and looks at me.

I kiss her gently, but then with delighted abandon. She reciprocates.

It doesn't go on indefinitely. To her surprise I'm the one to break it off.

To her greater surprise I stand up. I retrieve the glass and finish off what's left in it, then set it back on the table.

'I should go.'

No reason given. Other than an unstated one. That I've reached the same conclusion—there's little chance of it working out.

I find my jacket in the hall closet.

She's unsure what to say, except, 'Perhaps you should call a cab.'

There is that. That last shot of Laphroaig ran a bit long.

I take out my phone.

'Unless you want to stay the night.'

Shit.

I look up. 'I could.'

But I won't. I dial the number and talk.

If my self-control surprises me, it shouldn't. I work at trying not to let it show.

'A decision for another time,' I tell her. I open the door to exit before the cab could possibly have arrived. 'Good night.'

She raises her hand from the sofa but doesn't say anything.

I step out and close the door behind me. That was quick. Maybe too quick, who the hell knows.

Outdoors, the air has turned colder. Too early for leaves to fall, but there is a tree under the streetlight with a few showing a hint of red.

I open the front passenger seat of the cab, rather than sit in the back.

I asked the dispatcher for this particular driver. Despite the mask, he's a reminder of what first led me into criminal investigation.

'Ivo, my man, whataya at?'

'Good, Mr. Synard, good. Still hanging on.'

'That's good, Ivo.'

'COVID screwed up the plans, you know, but me and Ash are still going to get to Latvia. Eventually.'

'Patience, Ivo, it takes patience.' I like knowing the world's still spinning, that people hold fast when the going gets rough. 'We'll see, won't we, we'll see how it all works out.'

'How about you, Mr. Synard?'

'You know me, Ivo, Always surprised by what life has in store. Never bored.'

He smiles broadly. I do the same.

'That's the bright side, Ivo. And, you know, as they say, still trying to get my shit together.'

ALSO IN THIS SERIES

One for the Rock
Two for the Tablelands

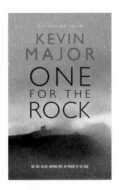